Bird Girl

MAUDIE SMITH

Orion
Children's Books

Bird Girl

First published in Great Britain in 2017
by Hodder and Stoughton

1 3 5 7 9 10 8 6 4 2

A CIP catalogue record for this book
is available from the British Library.

ISBN 978 1 4440 1562 1

Printed and bound in Great Britain by Clays Ltd, St Ives plc

The paper and board used in this book are from well-managed forests
and other responsible sources.

Orion Children's Books
An imprint of
Hachette Children's Group
Part of Hodder and Stoughton
Carmelite House
50 Victoria Embankment
London EC4Y 0DZ

An Hachette UK Company
www.hachette.co.uk

www.hachettechildrens.co.uk

To dreamers everywhere

Hold fast to dreams
for if dreams die
life is a broken-winged bird
that cannot fly.

From 'Dreams'
by Langston Hughes
(1902–1967)

One

The train doors opened again and Finch Field's chest fluttered with excitement. She could smell the sea at last!

"Your stop coming up."

The guard was handing out tickets on the other side of the aisle.

"Don't miss it now, will you?" she added, moving off down the carriage.

Finch smiled.

"I won't."

There was no way she could miss her stop. She'd been counting off the stations for hours, ever since

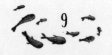

she'd waved goodbye to Mum and Dad. She'd watched impatiently as the view turned too slowly from houses and factories to fields and farms.

Now, on Finch's side of the train, there was only the sparkling sea, dotted with boats, and above it, a huge sheet of clear blue sky. Sunview-on-Sea was the next stop.

Finally!

Finch's fingers tingled. She'd been waiting for this trip all term – all year. Mum and Dad had worried about sending her off on her own for the whole summer, and Finch would miss them while they were abroad on the dig they had planned, but there was nowhere she'd rather spend the summer than Sunview-on-Sea.

And she wouldn't be on her own, she'd reminded them a thousand times. She would be with Granny Field and Philip at Hilltop House, her favourite place in the whole world.

She was just thinking about how much fun it would be seeing Philip, how he would wag his tail so hard that half his body moved with it, when something wet hit her neck.

"Oh!" She put up a hand to feel sticky liquid

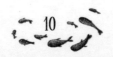

trickling down inside her collar. Where had that
come from?

A shadow stretched across the table in front of her.
Startled, she looked up to see a thin boy standing right
next to her, half in her seat, a drink carton crushed
in his hand. He leaned over, staring at her with dark,
expressionless eyes.

Finch stared back, pressing herself against the
window. She wonderered if he was going to squirt juice
at her again.

"That was a mistake. Not on purpose."

He spoke in a low voice and had a foreign accent she
didn't recognise.

"It was a slip of my hand."

Finch didn't know whether to believe him. The
trouble was, people were always doing things like that
to her: deliberately splashing their water at her, flicking
peas or pens in her direction. It happened at school all
the time. "Aren't you going to fly after it, Bird Girl?"
they would say as they sent rubbers sailing past her ear.
"What's the matter, Pecky, got your wings in a twist?"

She hadn't been expecting it to happen today.

"Accident," the boy said, as if he thought she

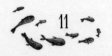

hadn't understood him the first time. He examined the crumpled drink carton in his hand. "The train swayed. Or perhaps I do not know my strength."

He didn't look strong. He had the thinnest arms Finch had ever seen.

"It's fine," she said, frowning and turning away, hoping he would leave her alone. Why did it have to happen now? This boy was spoiling the last and best part of her journey. She kept her eyes on the sea and the broadening yellowish beaches, but she knew he was still there; he had a noisy way of breathing.

He was probably staring at her hair. He was going to tease her about it. People often did, because it was tinged such an unusual shade of pink. They thought she dyed it, but she didn't, it had always been that way. It was the reason her parents had called her Finch in the first place, because her hair was the same soft pink as a chaffinch's breast.

She tensed, waiting for the boy's mocking comment, but all he said was, "Right. So long then, until next time."

"Mmm," Finch murmured as he walked away. She lifted her hair from where it had plastered itself to her neck. With a bit of luck there wouldn't be a next time.

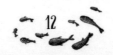

The train was already slowing down. She hurried to collect her things and put on her backpack, pulling the straps nice and tight so it would be comfortable to carry.

The train pulled to a halt and she waited for what seemed like ages for the lock to release, swinging the door wide as soon as it did.

"Bit of a gap at this one." The guard was there again. "Big jump. Mind how you go."

But Finch leaped down easily, landing lightly on the platform.

"Very nimble," said the guard. "Someone meeting you, is there?"

"Not really." Finch smiled. "But don't worry. I know exactly where I'm going."

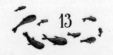

13

Two

Finch stood for a moment amidst the cheerful hubbub on the platform.

Families arriving for their holidays wheeled whirring cases at a great rate, talking excitedly. Families leaving for home scooped up straying toddlers and counted luggage. Doors slammed. Whistles blew. A train whizzed through on the opposite platform and the flowers that spilled out of the hanging baskets quivered like flickering orange stars. The afternoon sun sent a fan of golden rays across the station.

Above her, Finch heard the familiar call of the seagulls; she smiled up at them as they went gliding

14

over the old iron footbridge, white wings outstretched against a pure blue sky.

Sunview-on-Sea.

Finch breathed in its familiar sounds and smells. She was all alone on the busy platform, but that was what she had wanted. She had asked specially to be allowed to make her own way from the station, up through the little town to Hilltop House. She'd been looking forward to her arrival in Sunview so much, she wanted to be able to take it all in properly.

And because they knew that Sunview-on-Sea was the safest, happiest town in the country, her parents had agreed. Finch had promised to phone them as soon as she reached Granny Field's house.

She took one last look round the station. Her heart sank as she caught sight of the skinny boy again. He was sitting on the platform bench, a battered rucksack on his back, hugging two white carrier bags to his chest. He didn't seem to be with anyone either. He was staring into space, biting his fingernails. His dark eyes, Finch saw, were surrounded by purplish shadows, like bruises. His neck was scrawny inside his baggy jumper, and his cheeks were almost as pale as the carrier bags on

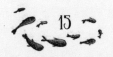
15

his lap, which shivered in the breeze. If Finch had been trying to draw a zombie she thought she might have drawn someone like him.

Before he could look up and speak to her again, Finch turned and marched down the platform. She had often imagined her arrival in Sunview – it had been her favourite thing to do – but there had never been a boy like this in the scenes her mind had conjured up for her. There had never been anything awkward or difficult. She hoped the boy wasn't staying in town. She hoped he was just waiting for a connecting train. She pushed all thoughts of him away and took off, dodging easily through the milling passengers and out onto the street.

"Someone's in a hurry."

Finch looked round. A dented van was waiting next to her, at the traffic lights. A young man leaned out of the open window, his jacket sleeve rolled up over his elbow to catch the sun. An array of brushes and spanners stuck out of his top pocket.

"How do, Finch?" he said with a grin.

"Hi, Dave," she said, going over at once. "How's the Down Under fund?"

Dave was Sunview-on-Sea's odd job man. Finch

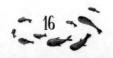

knew him well because he did all sorts of useful things for Granny Field. Dave worked all the hours he could. He was saving up for a trip to Australia.

"Coming along nicely, thank you for asking," he said. "I'll be stroking koala bears and laughing with kookaburras before you can say 'Surf's up!'"

Finch giggled.

"I'm off to paint some boat bottoms at the harbour," said Dave, pushing back his floppy fringe. "How about yourself?"

"Just arrived," Finch said, turning to show him her backpack. "I'm walking up to Granny Field's house."

"Lovely day for a stroll. Have fun!" Dave waved a tanned arm at her as the lights changed and he pulled away.

Finch waved back. She followed Dave's van at first, in the direction of the little harbour. But when she reached the bowling green – with its white pavilion and bright green grass, clipped so short it looked like carpet – she turned off, wove a path through the throng of sandy holidaymakers coming from the beach, and crossed the road.

She was striding up Middle Street when a toddler in

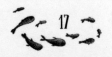

a spotty skirt tottered out of the play park and stood in front of her, putting her fingers in her mouth. It took Finch a moment to realise that she knew the little girl. It was Granny Field's neighbour, Delia.

"She wasn't walking last time you saw her, Finch, was she?"

Nikki, her mum, was standing nearby with a pushchair.

"No, she wasn't." Finch crouched down. "Hello, Delia," she said.

Delia looked at her seriously out of her round eyes. "Deel can walk anywhere she wants now. Can jump too. Look."

She paraded around in a circle and demonstrated a series of tiny jumps, puffing and grinning for all she was worth. Then she did one triumphant final stamp. "Tah dah!"

"Brilliant!" said Finch, giving Delia a clap. "Got to go. See you soon though."

"Yes, I hear you're expected up the hill. Finch is going to stay with Serena," Nikki explained to Delia. "Give my regards to your granny," she said.

"I will," Finch called back. She flitted up Middle Street, jumping happily from side to side across the

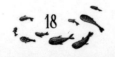

little stream that ran in a gully all the way down to the ocean.

She couldn't resist pausing at Sue's Souvenirs, to look at all the sea urchins and shells, glitter globes and key-rings and I ♥ Sunview-on-Sea mugs. Lots of people loved Sunview and bought Sue's mugs at the end of their holidays. *But no one loves it more than I do*, Finch thought as she gazed at the window display.

"Well, if it isn't young Finch!" The bell over the door clanged merrily and Sue herself came out of the shop, price stickers up her arms, dusters trailing from her trouser pockets. She gave Finch a huge hug.

"How are you?" Finch said, breathing in a gust of flowery scent.

"Busy busy!" said Sue. "But never mind. One of these days my prince will come! I'm sure of it. That's what keeps me going."

Finch smiled. Sue always said that about her prince.

"I hear you're with us for the whole summer. Won't that be a treat!"

"I should say so," agreed a gruff voice.

It was Fred from Fred's Fish on the other side of the street, in his stripy apron and straw boater.

"Saw you chatting with Sue here, Finch," he said, "so I left the fish to their own devices for a moment. Don't worry, though, I've told the haddock they're in charge of the sardines."

Finch giggled as he offered her his hand to shake. She loved Fred because whatever he said always had the beginning of a chuckle in it.

"Trust you saw the bowling green on your way up," he said. "How was it looking?"

"Absolutely perfect!" said Finch. When Fred wasn't in his fish shop he was down at the bowling green, mowing and rolling the grass into a flat green pancake.

"That's good," Fred said. "Because the county tournament's coming up and I'm planning to win it this year. Or if not this year, next year, or maybe the one after that. But it'll be my name inscribed on that silver trophy before too long."

"I bet it will, too," said Finch.

"'Course it will!" Sue laughed and shook out a duster. "Now come on, Fred. Enough of your dreams. Let's you and me get back to work. We're keeping Finch from her granny."

"Far be it from me to do that." Fred tipped his hat at

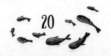

Finch and Sue.

Finch ran on. She was so pleased to see all her friends from Sunview-on-Sea. Apart from the growing Delia they looked exactly the same as the last time she had seen them, a whole year ago. Dave and Nikki, Sué and Fred. They were all so kind to her. She never wanted them to change.

As she passed the Conch Café she heard singing coming from a vent in the basement. The song was very pretty but she couldn't tell what it was about because whoever was singing was doing so in a foreign language. Finch guessed it must be Irena, the lady who had taken over the Conch Café a few months before. Granny Field had told her about that on the phone. Irena was letting out rooms, too, she said.

The Conch looked quite different now. It had been repainted pearly white and had puffy pink curtains flapping at its upstairs windows. The B&B sign in the front window said "No Vacancies" and the round tables inside were busy with cutlery and napkins and fresh flowers in little white vases.

The singing grew suddenly louder and a woman burst out of the door, tying a brightly coloured scarf

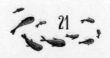

around her black hair. Her shoes clopped as she hurried down the hill, checking her watch and tutting, as if she was late for a meeting. A rich aroma of fresh baking and cinnamon wafted out of the café after her. The delicious smell seemed to give Finch fuel and she skipped up even the steepest part of the hill, turning left, away from the shops, and along the narrow lane that led to her destination. Hilltop House.

Philip must have caught her scent because she heard his first excited barks as soon as she turned the last corner. She couldn't see him, down behind the garden wall, but there was someone she could see.

Standing barefoot as always, on the slope of her garden, with her long white hair and skirt billowing in the breeze, waving and waving. Granny Field! Granny Field who was always laughing, Granny Field who listened to everything Finch said with her head on one side like a wise bird. Granny Field who had a clever knack of somehow making Finch feel that she wasn't so peculiar or so different from everyone else after all.

Finch rushed through the gate feeling the last cares and niggles of the school term fall away. "Granny Field!" she cried.

"Finch Field!" Granny cried back. "Well done, my darling! You're here and you're beautiful and you're right on time!"

They spun one another round and round until Finch felt their feet might almost leave the ground. And Philip barked his approval and wagged his stumpy tail.

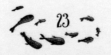

Three

"Here comes the strawberry!" Finch shouted, pointing up at the sky.

"Oh, yes," Granny Field set her cup of tea down on the bench, "and there's my favourite. The rainbow. Isn't it a beauty?"

They had spent the rest of the afternoon in the garden – Granny never went inside at all if she could help it. Now they were having supper out there, eating sweet, sharp blackcurrants straight off the bushes for dessert, and watching the first hot air balloons of the evening float over Sunview-on-Sea. Granny Field's garden was so high up it had the best view of the

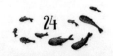

balloons. In fact it had the best view of everything – the town, the sea and the sky. That was why Granny Field liked it. Because she could see so much of the world. And she adored the world. She always said she could never get tired of it.

Finch loved watching the balloons go over. Sometimes they came in the early morning, almost before anyone was up, with only the occasional hiss and burst of flame announcing their arrival. Other times they came in the evening – stately blobs of blue and red, black and gold, sailing across the sky like ships leading in the sunset.

"I bet it'll be the stars and stripes next," she said. They were playing the balloon game. They both knew all the balloons well and they had to guess which one would appear next. Whoever had the most correct guesses got to do a victory dance. Philip would scamper after the winner as they danced all the way from the bench down to The Empress – the tallest tree in the garden – and back again. Finch was winning easily this evening because Granny Field wasn't doing all that much guessing; she was too busy filling Finch in on what she had in mind for the garden. It was her dream

to have the best, most glorious garden in England. It was so beautiful, Finch thought it probably already was the best garden in England, with its waving pink and orange spires and its sunflowers as big as frying pans. But Granny Field wanted it to be even better, and just now she was planning a huge pond.

"It's going to be right here," she said, sweeping an arm at an area of lawn. "With water lilies and marsh marigolds and a million frogs and fish! What shape do you think it should be, Finch? Figure of eight? Or more like a giant pear? Dave's going to help me dig it out. Will you help too, love? It can be our summer project."

Finch nodded eagerly. "Of course I will. But aren't you going to make your guess now, Granny?"

"Oh yes," said Granny Field, "Let's see. The next balloon. I say it'll be the . . ." She put her head back to examine the sky. "Cloud," she said abruptly.

"What? There isn't a cloud balloon, is there?" There certainly hadn't been one with clouds on it the previous summer. But following Granny Field's gaze, Finch saw it wasn't a balloon she was looking at. It was a cloud. A real one. Not a puffy, white one, like a sheep or a cauliflower, but a flatter, darker, more unusual one.

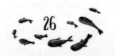

It sprawled across the sky like a heavy rug, travelling slowly but surely along, behind the hot air balloons.

"That's a funny looking cloud," Finch said. "Isn't it, Granny?"

Granny Field didn't answer. She was very still, staring at the cloud, as if she was mesmerised by it.

"Granny!" Finch cried. "Watch what you're doing!"

Granny Field broke away from the cloud and looked down at her skirt which was trickling with purple. She had been clenching her fist so tightly she had squeezed the blackcurrants of their juice.

She shook her head and licked her dripping hand. "Silly me. I must be going daft!"

Finch laughed. "It's only a cloud," she said.

Granny looked up again for a moment, as if to make sure. Then she laughed too. "Of course it is," she said. "Come on now, let's finish our game. I reckon it'll be your turn to do the victory dance tonight, Finch!"

When they went back inside the tall old house, Granny Field put her arm round Finch, pulling her in

tight so that Finch felt their bones pressed together. She and Granny Field were both bony and skinny. They were the only ones in the family that were. They had the same type of hair too, the type that fluffed up like thistledown and wouldn't stay flat, however hard you brushed it. Finch liked taking after her Granny Field. She wasn't a bit like her dad. Carl Field was solidly built, just like Grandpa Field had been. Finch's mum had broad shoulders too, whereas Finch was slender and slight. Sometimes people wondered that the three of them were related. But it made perfect sense if you knew Granny Field.

Finch rang her parents one more time to say goodnight and wish them a good trip. They were both geologists and would be spending the next three weeks in Africa, studying the ground. Finch didn't know what kind of job she would have when she left school, but she didn't think she would follow in her parents' footsteps. She didn't particularly like poring over the earth the way they did. She preferred being up high, climbing trees and looking out at the world.

"You'll miss your mum and dad," Granny Finch said.

"Yes," Finch agreed. "But not too much. Not now that I'm here."

28

"Sweetest of dreams, my Finch," Granny said, when they parted on the landing.

As she brushed her teeth, Finch thought how funny it was that people wished one another sweet dreams. She had exactly the same dream every night. Nothing she did ever changed it. Having identical dreams seemed normal to her. She had only recently discovered that it wasn't normal for everyone.

Finch had always been different. No one else at school had pink hair like her, and she was so small she was often mistaken for a child from one of the younger classes. But these were only physical differences. They didn't explain why she didn't fit in. She had tried to make friends. Encouraged by Mum and Dad she had invited girls home for tea. Sometimes she had been invited back to their houses. But no friendship had ever really got going. It wasn't that Finch didn't share the same interests as the others, she was just always at odds with them somehow.

Then one day, out of the blue, Mrs Bennett had asked what everyone dreamed of doing in the future. The others had all said they dreamed of being inventors or marine biologists, footballers, actors or celebrities.

But Finch had said simply that her dream was to fly. Not like a pilot, she'd explained, not in an aeroplane or a para-glider or anything like that. But just as she was, using her arms for wings. "It's all I ever dream of," she'd said. "It's the only thing I want, in the whole wide world!"

There had been a brief silence. Someone sniggered and then everyone fell about laughing.

"Well, what an interesting ambition!" Mrs Bennett had said. "Finch is quite the little bird girl, isn't she? Of course, at this school, we're always pleased to see our fledglings – I mean our *children* – go out and spread their wings!" She didn't mean to be cruel but her joke had only encouraged more scornful laughter.

Finch couldn't understand why the others all thought her dream was so funny. Why did something so natural to her seem so ridiculous to them, and make them so unkind?

"I'll do it one day, too," she'd said, glaring round. "I'll show you!" They had laughed even more. Finch still hadn't heard the last of it.

Bird Girl! Feathers for Brains! Beak Features!

The others never seemed to tire of calling her names

or telling her to fly after things they threw up in the air – crisp packets or chewed blobs of still warm gum.

She'd minded at first, very much. But then she'd trained herself not to rise to the bait, not even when the little missiles they threw hit her, or when the chewing gum got stuck in her hair and had to be cut out.

The distance that already existed between Finch and her classmates increased. She had no-one she could call a friend, and she was often alone at break times. She started taking herself off deliberately, pretending she preferred being on her own. She was determined not to let the others see how much she cared.

And she was determined not to be humiliated again. She'd resolved never again to tell anyone what she dreamed about night after night after night. And she hadn't. Not even Granny Field.

But Finch couldn't have stopped herself from having the flying dream, even if she'd wanted to. Not that she did want to. The dream was part of her. Sometimes her dream seemed more real to her than the life she lived in the daytime.

"I can't help it," she whispered, snuggling down under the patchwork quilt. "It's what makes me me."

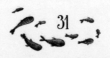

And she closed her eyes, ready for the flight she knew sleep would bring.

Four

When Finch woke up, she thought it must be very early. The sun wasn't streaming in yet, the way it always did in the mornings in Sunview, lighting up the armies of wonky homemade pots and vases which filled Granny Field's shelves. So she was surprised when she looked at the little clock on her bedside table, to find it was nearly nine o'clock.

It was the cloud's fault. It was still there when she opened the curtains, in the same place as last night. Only it looked bigger now, spreading out over Sunview-on-Sea like a dark stain of ink. And it was doing a perfect job of blocking out the sun.

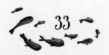

"There you are!" Granny Field was outside with all the breakfast things and her garden sketch book. She closed it at once when she saw Finch, and started showering cereal into a bowl for her. "Come on, sleepy head. We've errands to run in the town, and you haven't even been down to the sea yet. You do want to go to the beach today, don't you?"

"Oh yes!" Finch hesitated. "Although it might not be the best beach day." She nodded at the cloud.

"Every day's a good beach day in Sunview," Granny Field said firmly. "Isn't that right, Philip?" Philip wagged his tail. Granny didn't even glance at the cloud. She seemed to be deliberately ignoring it. "Look sharp, my lovely!" she said, splashing milk over the cereal. "It's high time for the sea!"

Granny chatted away as normal on the walk down the hill, but Finch couldn't help noticing the cheerfully coloured houses that lined the street looked duller than usual, almost as if they were shocked to find themselves under such a heavy cloud. *No wonder*, Finch thought. Sunview was always warm and baked in sunshine, even when it was raining everywhere else. Granny Field claimed the town had its own private weather system,

but Finch thought it was more like magic.

Normally there would have been lots of holidaymakers ambling along, but there was hardly anyone else about. They did see Nikki and Delia, on their way back up the hill. Delia was crying hard, dragging her feet, and Nikki was looking exhausted.

"Oh dear! Poor Delia. Anything we can do?" Granny asked.

Nikki shook her head. "It's been like this all morning. She keeps saying she's lost something, but she won't tell me what. To be honest, I'm not even sure she knows herself."

"Perhaps she's sickening," Granny said. She patted Delia's heaving shoulders. "Are you catching a cold, sweetheart?"

Delia looked up at Granny Field and Finch saw a fresh set of tears spring from her eyes. "Want . . . jump . . . my . . . wellies!" she managed to gasp, before another volley of hiccupping sobs prevented her from speaking again.

"But you haven't got any wellies!" Nikki sounded exasperated. "And it hasn't rained for weeks. Come on. Serena's right, you must be ill. I'd better get you home."

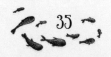

"No!" Delia shrieked and stood her ground, until Nikki took hold of one of her clenched little fists and pulled her away.

"Will she be all right?" Finch didn't like seeing Delia so upset, or Nikki for that matter.

"I'm sure she will," Granny said. "But it's funny, because Delia's such a happy little soul as a rule. Whatever's bothering her has taken a firm hold." She glanced at the sky and sucked a finger thoughtfully.

They carried on down Middle Street in silence until Granny stopped outside the fishmongers. "How about some nice fresh fish? We'll ask Fred to put it aside and collect it on the way home. Granny's cod dippers for tea?"

Finch nodded enthusiastically. Granny Field was a great cook and cod dippers were one of her specialities.

Fred was behind the counter as usual, in his familiar blue and white striped apron and the brimmed hat with the plastic daffodil. While Granny ordered, Finch hovered in the doorway with Philip. She couldn't help smiling. Any moment now Fred would take his pencil from behind his ear and ask if she fancied taking this excellent opportunity of securing the autograph of the

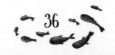

future County Crown Bowling Champion. It could be worth a few quid in years to come, he always assured her. Finch already had a small pile of paper bags at home, all of them signed *Frederick Stanley Jenkins* in a flourishing hand. She fully expected to get another bag for her collection today.

But Fred only nodded when he saw her. "Finch," he said. He wrapped up Granny's fish. "Three pounds eighty, thank you, Serena." Granny paid and left the shop, and that was all.

"Fred didn't say hello to me properly." Finch tried not to sound offended.

"I know," Granny said. "What's got his goat, I wonder? Never mind. Let's go and see Souvenir Sue. She's always in a good mood." They hopped over the little stream. Finch went first, eagerly pushing open the door of the gift shop.

She couldn't see Sue to begin with. Usually she was flying round the shop, doing several things all at once: taking money, filling in order forms, dusting, straightening postcards in racks, perching on stepladders to take down hanging mobiles made of driftwood. And she was always chatting – either to

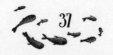

customers or on the phone.

Sue wasn't chatting to anyone today, though. They found her by a display of Sunview-on-Sea coffee mugs, re-stocking it slowly, mug by mug, sitting on a stool while she worked. Finch couldn't remember ever having seen her sitting down before. She didn't even turn round, despite the loud jangle of the doorbell that had announced their arrival.

"Morning, Sue," Granny said.

"Sorry, loves," Sue said, turning at last and wiping a bleary eye. "Didn't hear you come in."

"You all right?" Granny asked. "You seem tired."

"I feel tired," Sue admitted. "It's taking me three times longer than usual to do anything today. I've been doing these blimmin' mugs all morning. To tell you the truth, I'm properly fed up."

"Never mind," Finch said, trying to be helpful. "Perhaps your prince will be here soon."

"A prince? Come for me?" Sue rolled her eyes. She picked at the worn knees of her corduroy trousers and sighed. "I don't think so, Finch. I'm past all that. Too old for romance now."

"Never!" exclaimed Granny Field. "No-one's too old

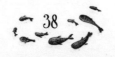

for romance, Sue. Not even me, probably!"

But Sue was already unwrapping the next mug. She hung it carefully on a hook, and dipped her hand into the cardboard box for another, carrying on with her work as if Finch and Granny Field had already left the shop.

"What's the matter with everyone today?" Finch said. There were no children at the play park, clambering on the whale climbing frame. There were no holidaymakers heading for the harbour or the beach. "Where are all the people?"

As they passed the bowling green Finch noticed a few jagged weeds had pushed their way up in the smooth green grass. Fred wouldn't like that. He'd be down there as soon as the fish shop shut to pull them up.

"Do you think it's the cloud?" Finch knew sunlight was important for people. You needed a little of it every day for healthy skin and it made you happy.

Granny frowned. "Why would it be?" she said. "It's only a cloud after all." Then she smiled at Finch. "We're not going to let some silly old cloud make us feel down in the dumps, are we, Finch?"

"Of course we're not," Finch agreed.

"Anyway," said Granny, "I dare say it'll be gone by tomorrow. Sunview and clouds are two things that just do not go together."

She spoke firmly, as if she was scolding the cloud for being there. Finch was about to ask her what if it *wasn't* gone by the next day when Philip started pulling on the lead. He'd spotted Dave in the harbour. And Dave kept dog treats in his jacket pockets, just for Philip.

As soon as he saw them Dave stopped painting the hull of the boat he was working on, grabbed his jacket from the harbour rail and sent a treat spinning into the air for Philip to catch. A ten pound note floated out of his pocket to the ground.

"Whoops! That's one for the Down Under fund," Dave said, picking it up and tucking it back in. "Better take care of it, eh, Finch?"

At least Dave was in a good mood. Finch was relieved to see that.

"How much longer until you have enough money?"

Dave made a face. "Hard to say. I'll have to tot it up. I'll get to Australia eventually though. Shall I send you a postcard when I do?"

"Yes, please!" Finch said. "One with a koala bear on

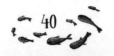

the front, or a kookaburra bird!"

Dave stuck up a thumb. "You're on."

Then he and Granny started discussing the jobs
Granny wanted him to help with in her garden. As well
as the pond she was planning, she was going to plant
half a dozen peach trees against the sunniest wall of the
house. She wanted Dave to help dig the planting holes.

"I see it quite clearly in my dreams," she said, her
eyes dancing merrily. "In a few summers' time we'll be
sitting out, eating soft ripe peaches with so much juice
in them, it'll be dribbling down our chins!"

"Sounds good to me." Dave winked at Finch.

Finch winked back and left them to it. She wanted to
see the sea. She ran down the slipway, skipping her way
over the big stones, leaping over the pebbly stream and
onto the beach.

It was a summer's day, right in the middle of the
holiday season. But the beach was completely deserted.
That wasn't right. She gazed up at the cloud and shook
her fist at it.

"Cloud, cloud, go away," she chanted. "Don't come
again another day!"

It must have been her imagination, but as she spoke

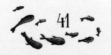

41

the cloud seemed to hover and drop a little lower, and Finch was seized by a horrible feeling that while she was looking up at it, the cloud was also looking down at her.

Five

Finch ran towards the water. It felt odd, knowing hers were the only footprints in the smooth, flat sand. The sea cleared the beach every day. It swept away all the sandcastles and moats and hopscotch games. But for once, no one had undone any of its work. The sea wouldn't have much tidying up to do this evening. And that didn't feel like a good thing.

Finch slipped off her pumps and paddled. The shallowest of waves washed gently over her feet. The sea was very still, dark and grey. But it was only in Sunview that it looked like that: from the beach, Finch had a good view up and down the coast, and she could

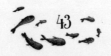

see stretches of bright blue and green water to either side. Other beaches glowed a warm yellow where the sun was getting through. But there wasn't a glimpse of sun in Sunview. The cloud had the town wrapped in deep shade.

A queue of cars jammed the coast road. All the holidaymakers were leaving, in search of sunnier places. Finch didn't understand it. How could so many people turn their backs on Sunview so quickly?

"Some people have no staying power!" she said out loud, trying to sound like Granny Field to make herself feel better. But she couldn't help counting the departing cars, all full of disloyal people. She was still counting them when something sharp hit her on the back of her leg.

A pebble ricocheted off her calf and plopped into the water.

"Ow!"

She spun round.

The boy from the train was perching on a boulder just a few metres behind her. So he hadn't left town after all.

"What did you do that for?" she demanded. She wondered how long he'd been watching her, and how

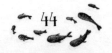

he'd got there without her noticing.

The boy opened his hand, revealing several flattish pebbles. "I'm teaching myself to skim the stones. It is much more difficult than it looks." He spoke in a stilted way and his voice was rough and husky, as if there was rust trapped somewhere deep in his chest.

"It's not *that* difficult," Finch said indignantly. "You must be a terrible aim. There's a whole empty beach here, and you go and hit the one person who happens to be on it!"

"Sorry. I did not mean to hit you so hard."

"So you did mean to hit me!"

"No. Yes. Not exactly. I did want to have your attention for a minute." The boy gazed at her with his hooded eyes. Then he said, "Rose pink."

"Don't call me that!" Finch snapped, putting a hand to her hair. She didn't need another nickname — what with *Pecky*, *Feather-brain* and *Bird Girl*, she had plenty already. "My name's not Rose Pink and you shouldn't throw stones!" Angry, she turned on her heel and started back towards the harbour.

"Hey!" the boy said. "Wait, please. I wanted to tell you something."

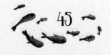

Finch kept walking.

"It's important. I want to tell you to take care of your dreams!"

Finch stopped, a chill spreading through her chest. Why say a thing like that? She'd seen this boy only once before in her life, she was sure of it. So what could he know about her dream? Her secret? She shook her head. Nothing! He couldn't know anything about her. It was impossible, she was letting her imagination run away with her.

Still, she felt an urgent need to put as much distance between herself and this boy as she could. She broke into a sprint, running towards Granny Field who she could see sitting on the harbour wall, looking out to sea.

She turned back once, when she reached the jetty. The boy was standing up now, tall and spindly on the boulder. He wasn't looking at her any longer. His thin arms were raised above his head, pointing towards the cloud. He looked as if he was talking to it.

Finch shivered and ran on up the steps. "Let's go," she said.

Granny Field didn't answer at first. She seemed to be deep in thought, one hand pressed to her mouth.

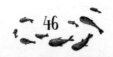

"Granny? Are you OK?"

"Oh. Of course." Granny Field let her hand drop and used it to dig a couple of biscuits out of her skirt pocket. She passed one to Finch. "I just got caught up in an old memory of mine, that's all." She nibbled the corner of her biscuit. "It happens to us old folks from time to time, you know."

"You're not old." Finch linked arms with Granny Field as she got up from the wall. "You'll never be old."

Granny Field chuckled. "Make a friend down there, did you?" she asked, nodding towards the beach.

"No, I did not!" Finch bent to rub her leg which was still smarting from the pebble. "That is the rudest boy I've ever met. Do you know who he is?"

"White as a sheet too, isn't he?" said Granny. "Could be Irena's nephew. I heard he was coming over. Irena said she was going to take him in at the Conch Café. Give his parents a break."

"Why do they need a break? From him?"

"Yes, I suppose so. He doesn't go to school at the moment apparently. And they've got their hands full. Irena said she'd have him for the summer."

So she'd been right to avoid the boy, Finch thought.

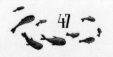

Maybe he hadn't followed her here, but her instincts about him had been correct. If he didn't go to school he must have done something really bad – bad enough to be suspended, maybe even expelled.

"He's called Tomas, I think," said Granny.

"He told me to take care of my dreams," said Finch, indignant all over again. "Why would he say a thing like that?"

"Did he? How curious." Granny pondered for a moment as if she was giving it serious thought. Then she smiled. "I'm sure it's nothing, maybe just a saying where he comes from. A sort of well wish."

"Or a sort of threat," Finch said under her breath, glaring up at the cloud. She wanted the cloud gone, and she wanted the boy gone too. Between them they were spoiling the town. Sunview-on-Sea was her perfect precious place and she wanted it to go back to normal.

Six

The cloud didn't leave though. It settled itself lower and even more firmly over the town, its edges folding down like a giant unwanted duvet. It settled so low it almost touched the top of The Empress, Granny's tree – the highest point in the town.

The forecast was for bright and sunny weather all over the county, but it was neither bright nor sunny in Sunview and as the days passed, more and more holidaymakers left town. The signs at the bed and breakfast hotels changed from 'No Vacancies' to 'Vacancies' and when Finch passed the Conch Café there was no more sweet singing to hear. There were no

more delicious baking smells either, just the sour reek of cigarette smoke.

The only people left in Sunview now were the ones who lived there all year round, and most of them trudged about, muttering to themselves in a bewildered way, as if they had lost something but couldn't quite remember what.

Each morning Finch woke to hear the hiss of the hot air balloons. She always rushed to her window hoping to see them, but she never could. The air clamped beneath the cloud had grown still and stale, and the wind blew the balloons higher, away from the town. They were completely hidden by the cloud and Finch could only imagine them breezing along in the fresh bright sky she knew still lay above.

Granny Field seemed determined to ignore the cloud altogether, and threw herself more energetically than ever into working on her garden. Finch was relieved she hadn't succumbed to the strange mood that had taken over most of the townspeople, but she couldn't help noticing that even Granny Field was behaving a little oddly. Whenever Finch raised the topic of the cloud she shrugged it off at once, saying

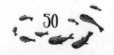

50

it was sure to be gone soon. Then she would smartly change the subject.

And in the evenings Granny Field was quieter than usual. She spent more and more time on the garden bench with her book, scribbling in the back of it. Once Finch came out and stood behind her and saw she had drawn a series of roundish shapes.

"Are you sketching the pond?"

Granny Field jumped and closed the book. "You startled me!"

"Sorry," Finch said. "Have you decided on a shape yet? Is Dave coming to dig it out?"

"Oh, well. The pond." Granny Field smoothed the cover of her sketchbook, which as far as Finch could see was perfectly smooth already. "I can't seem to make my mind up."

Finch frowned. Granny Field was very decisive as a rule. She made decisions more quickly than Finch could snap her fingers. She sat down next to her. "It'll come to you soon though, won't it, Granny?"

Granny Field leaned out and planted a kiss in Finch's hair. "It will," she said. "Of course it will. Everything comes right in the end."

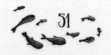

51

Finch wanted to believe Granny Field was right, but Sunview-on-Sea felt more like a ghost town every day. When she took Philip out for his walks, Finch often ran all the way to the beach without stopping. It was too upsetting to linger anywhere for long. There were too many disappointing sights, like the shutters pulled down over the window at Sue's Souvenirs, or Fred's precious bowling green, where the weeds, far from being pulled up, were completely taking over.

One morning Finch was so intent on getting away from the things that troubled her in town that she went much further than she'd meant to. Before she knew it she had crossed the length of the beach and was climbing the steps that led the way onto the coastal path.

When she reached the top of the steps, she stood panting, taking in the view. The six hills ahead of her were named The Three Camels because they looked like three distinct pairs of camel humps. If she half-shut her eyes she could imagine them as a trio of gigantic camels walking in a train, next to the sea. The farthest Camel was bright green and bathed in sunshine, but the nearer two were cast in shade. Finch glanced up at the cloud, then strode along quickly, suddenly determined to reach a bright spot on the coastal path.

Philip pulled ahead, excited to be on such a long walk. Finch let him off the lead and he ran in front of her, investigating, snuffing at rabbit holes and interesting clumps of bristly heather. Finch ran too, spreading her arms out wide, going so fast her feet barely touched the ground. Just a little further and she was sure they would break out from under the cloud. She longed to be free of its strange weight.

"Ruff-ruff. Ruff-ruff-ruff!"

Philip was leaping back and forth by a tiny brick building. Finch had seen the building before. Granny Field had shown it to her once. It was an old wartime look-out post, called a pill box. She went over and crouched down at its darkened entrance. Philip was barking away at it, as if he had something cornered in there.

"Silly dog," she said, holding onto his collar. "That rabbit will have escaped as soon as it heard you. There's

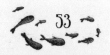

53

nothing there now."

"Actually, there is." A voice echoed in the dark.

Finch jumped and fell backwards into a bush of prickly gorse.

She stared as a pair of trainers emerged, soles-first, from the pill box. They were followed by rolled-down yellowish socks, thin pale legs, baggy brown shorts, a dark jumper, and the rest of the boy she now knew was called Tomas.

"It looks as if I must say sorry yet again," he said, fixing her with his charcoal eyes. "Sorry for alarming you. Are you OK?"

Finch scrambled out of the bush. "Of course I'm OK!"

The boy's eyes narrowed and she suspected him of trying not to smile.

"I don't see what's so funny." Finch smoothed down her skirt. "And don't you go calling me Rose Pink again either," she said as the boy opened his mouth to speak. "You'll only make things worse."

"I didn't."

"Yes, you did. I heard you."

"No. I wasn't calling you Rose Pink," Tomas insisted. "I was just observing that is the colour of your hair.

54

I learned all the colours you see, in English, before I came. Sea green, egg-yolk yellow, rose pink."

"Oh, I see." Finch folded her arms, feeling a bit silly. "Well. Sorry," she said reluctantly, to show she realised she'd jumped to the wrong conclusion. "Anyway, my name's Finch. Finch Field. And yours is Tomas."

Tomas just nodded, watching as she pulled thorns from her arms, which reminded her that she was still annoyed with him. "What were you doing in there, anyway? You've done something wrong again, haven't you? Go on, tell me. Who are you hiding from?"

Tomas's face was serious now. "I thought it might have come and taken your dreams already," he said. "But I see you are still safe."

"What?" Finch said, ignoring the odd little quiver his words sent through her. "Of course I'm safe."

"But your dreams are not." Tomas nodded up at the cloud. "It's been taking them all you see, one by one, from the people of the town."

"What has?" Finch said. "The cloud?" She screwed up her face in disbelief.

"Not the cloud, Finch," Tomas replied, and his dark gaze seemed to flow right through her. "The cloud

monster."

Finch nearly laughed. "Cloud monster?" she said. "There's no such thing. Monsters don't exist!"

She grabbed Philip and put him on his lead. But Tomas wasn't put off.

"This monster exists," he said quietly. "It does. I've seen it with my own eyes. I saw it come to the Conch Café. It came on my first night here and stole my aunt's dream of opening a bakery. It took it right out of her head. All the raisin and rye cakes, the potato breads. Everything. The next day she was completely different. Dull as old water from a ditch. Without joy, and forgetting things. She's been the same way ever since."

"You're . . . you're mad," Finch said. "You're making it up."

But something kept her from turning away completely. Tomas's description of Irena reminded her of the way Fred and Sue and the other townspeople were behaving. They were dull and joyless too. It couldn't be a monster taking their dreams away, though. Of course it couldn't. But she wished she had a different explanation for what was going on.

"Wait a minute," she said. "How come you know

about the monster, and no one else does? How come you're the only one who's seen it? And if it is taking everyone's dreams, like you say, why didn't it take *your* dream too?"

Tomas didn't seem thrown by her question. He didn't behave as if she'd caught him out. "I see it because I stay awake," he said. "I don't sleep like other people, Finch Field." Grunting with the effort, he swung himself up and sat on the mossy cushion on top of the pill box. "I'm an insomniac."

"A what?"

"It means I can't sleep properly — never more than a few minutes at once anyway. And that's not long enough to have a proper dream, so I don't think the monster can hurt me. I did try telling Aunt Irena about it but she told me I was crazy. Everyone else here would say the same, I'm sure. But you. You seemed different. I thought you might *be* different." He paused to pull at some heather growing by his feet. "Unfortunately, I was wrong."

"Definitely," Finch said. "You're wrong about me and about everything else. Monsters don't exist. You're just making up stories to scare people. You shouldn't do

things like that." She pulled Philip away. "Come on," she said. "Time to go."

"I thought we could be a team, you see," Tomas persisted. "We could be the monster hunters. One person can't defeat a monster on their own. No one should try to do such things alone." He raised his hands. "After all, who wants to do everything alone?"

"I do," Finch said at once. "I do everything alone. I like it like that. And anyway," she shook her head at her him, "this is a pointless argument because I've already told you, there is no monster!"

She started off back along the coast path towards Sunview, yanking the reluctant Philip behind her.

Tomas still wouldn't stop talking. "It knows when you're in your deepest sleep," he called after her. He was coughing a bit now. "It comes in through the windows. I've seen it snake through tiny gaps. It's a very hungry monster. Watch out for it," he shouted and his voice rasped. "I'm warning you. Watch out for your dreams!"

"Stop it!" Finch shouted back. "It's not true. None of it. It's not true!" She ran on and tried to blot the upsetting words from her thoughts.

"Hurry up, Philip," she said. For some reason she was suddenly very anxious to be back at Hilltop House. "Granny Field will be wondering where we've got to."

Seven

Everything was very quiet when Finch reached
the gate at Hilltop House. Eerily quiet.

"Granny!" she called. "I'm back!"

No one answered.

Six new little trees with light pink blossoms leaned
against the house, but the garden was deserted. Granny
was always outside but now she was nowhere to be seen.

"Granny!" Finch cried out, suddenly very alarmed.
"Granny!"

"There you are at last! Thought you'd got lost."
Granny Field walked round the side of the house,
puffing a little and smiling, a heavy watering can in each

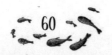

hand. "Come and see my new peach trees."

Finch was so relieved to see her, she ran and hugged her hard.

"Hey, silly, this is for the peaches, not my feet!" Granny Field chuckled as water sploshed over their toes.

"Was Dave here earlier?" Finch asked. "Was he . . . okay?"

"Fit as a fiddle," Granny said. "Same as every day. He dug my holes and went off to get some more painting done."

"And the pond? Is he coming to do that soon? Have you settled on a shape?"

"Yes, I have. Dave's going to make a start on it tomorrow."

"Oh, good." Finch sighed and pressed her face against Granny's shoulder, breathing in the familiar scent of lemon soap and long grass. She felt her heartbeat slowly return to normal.

"Do you believe in monsters?" she said after a moment.

Granny Field set down her watering cans. "Monsters?" she said. "What? Like vampires and dragons, you mean?"

Finch nodded.

"Who's been putting ideas into your head?" Granny smiled and cupped Finch's face in her hands. "I do not believe in monsters," she said firmly. "And nor should you." She looked up at the cloud then and said, "There's no such thing as monsters, and that's one thing I do know." She sounded stern, as if she was talking not just to Finch, but to the sky itself, almost as if she was challenging it to contradict her.

"Now then." She patted Finch's shoulders. "Are you going to help me water in my peaches, or not?"

Finch felt better after that. Pouring puddles of water around each newly planted tree was satisfying, and calmed her somehow.

When it came to bedtime, though, she began to worry again. Granny Field had been reassuring, but as she wriggled into her nightie, the words that echoed in her mind were not Granny's. They were Tomas's.

Take care of your dreams.

His warnings seemed to follow her about. She could feel them in the rhythm of her tooth-brushing. She could hear them in the last glugs of the water easing away down the plughole, and in the creaks her feet

made on the old wooden floorboards.

Watch out! Watch out for your dreams.

Supposing what Tomas had said was true and people really were having their dreams taken away by a monster, how long could it be before it visited Hilltop House? As far as Finch could tell, there were only a few people acting normally in the town now. She and Granny were two of them. What if they were next in line?

She was relieved when she heard the familiar scratch of claws and Philip nudged open her bedroom door.

"We're not afraid of any so-called cloud monsters, are we?" she said to him.

He wagged his stubby tail.

"Don't worry," Finch said. "You can sleep with me tonight." She sat stroking him on her lap for a while – somehow she didn't feel like getting into bed.

"I tell you what," she said to Philip. "We'll lay some traps, shall we? Just in case." Her eyes wandered around the room as she considered what sort of traps a cloud monster might fall into.

She settled for some tall clay pots, lots of oddments of knitting wool from Granny's craft basket and a few of Grandpa Field's old walking sticks – Grandpa Field had

died several years earlier but Granny still kept his sticks in the bucket by the front door. Finch arranged the pots around her bed, poking the sticks into the taller ones, and then looping long strands of wool over everything until she and Philip were sitting on the bed, hemmed in by pottery vases, pencil pots, candle-holders and walking sticks, all criss-crossed with a tangle of multi-coloured wool. Now, if anything came near her in the night, Finch was sure it would have to knock something over before it reached her. At least then she would be alerted to whatever it was.

She kept rolling over in bed, checking the clock at regular intervals until well after midnight. She thought she would never sleep. She wondered whether this was what being an insomniac was like. If so, it was exhausting. No wonder Tomas was so pale and had such dark rings beneath his eyes.

She must have fallen asleep eventually, though, because when she woke with a start and opened her eyes wide, the clock hands were standing at half past two. She was disoriented for a moment because she had been wrenched right out of the heart of her dream. She had been flying free, floating almost, letting the wind

do the work as she coasted high over miles of green and yellow fields. Now her body felt heavy and clumsy, as if it had been dropped from a height and had thudded roughly into the bed.

Something had interrupted the dream, cutting it short. Something had woken her. But what?

"Sssssssss."

Finch jumped. Something was hissing in the dark. She thought of the hot air balloons, but balloons never flew in the dead of night. Then she thought it might be Philip sighing in his sleep, but it wasn't him either. She could feel his body, tense and alert against her back. He was awake too. Wide awake. He growled when they both heard a clatter of wood and pottery hitting the bare floorboards.

In the dark, Finch froze, listening.

"Granny," she whispered. "Is that you?"

More hissing. Louder this time, and more insistent. Someone was definitely in the room.

And it wasn't Granny Field.

Eight

Trying to prevent her arm from shaking, Finch reached out and clicked on the bedside light. She flinched and clutched Philip to her as she saw what she had trapped in her snare.

Caught amongst the wool lay the most terrible creature. Its pale, flailing body seemed to have no particular form at all, but moved and bulged about, swelling and shrinking by turns. It seemed to have no arms or legs, just a ghostly body which it thrashed in all directions as it tried to free itself from the tangled woolly trap. Although it had no limbs, it did have a head. A horrible one with waving antennae on top, and

a long trunk-like nose. Sucking sounds came from the nose and Finch felt the ends of her hair fly up and the flimsy material of her nightie ripple, as if she was being pulled towards the creature.

It lurched suddenly and reared upwards, revolving its head. Finch saw not one, but three pairs of milk-white eyes, all of which rolled and roved around the room.

Finch was terrified. She pushed herself up against the wall, with Philip trembling in her arms.

"What are you?" she managed to stammer, wishing she could somehow press herself right through the wall and away. "Why are you here? What do you want?"

She could see at once that asking such questions was pointless, for although the creature had numerous blank eyes, it had no ears and no mouth. It could neither hear nor speak.

But the answer to one of Finch's questions was right in front of her. The creature's colourless body was virtually transparent and the contents of its stomach were clear to see. A rolling wave of surf curled itself over a brown bird with flashes of blue and turquoise plumage. The poor thing was desperately trying to fly.

Tumbling beneath the bird was a furry grey creature with fluffy ears.

Dave's koala bear!

Finch knew at once that she was looking at Dave's dream of Down Under. The creature must have come from Dave's flat. It had been there and hoovered up his dream. It must have sucked up the wave, the kookaburra and the koala whole, all at once.

And now it was here.

Philip barked, shrill and scared.

Finch's heart leaped. The creature was squirming loose.

"Get away!" she cried, standing on the bed and holding the quilt up as a shield. "Don't you come near me!"

The creature was completely free now. It towered over her, examining her with its awful eyes, sniffing at her with its hideous nose. The flimsy quilt was no defence at all. Finch closed her eyes. Shaking, she pressed her hands against the wall, waiting for the strike.

But nothing happened.

She heard Philip jump from the bed and growl, as if he was feeling a little braver. Was the monster leaving

them alone after all? She dared to open her eyes.

The creature wasn't hovering above her any longer but it wasn't making for the window either. Instead it had found a gap in the door and was pouring itself out onto the landing.

"Granny Field!" Finch hurled herself off the bed, grabbed one of Grandpa Field's walking sticks and sped across the floor.

She charged out of the room just in time to see the monster slither right under Granny Field's bedroom door. Finch burst in after it but it was already swarming over Granny's sleeping head. It clamped its trunk over her ear where it gripped like a leech. Finch wanted to rush at the monster and rip it away. She wanted to hit it with the stick. But she was frozen, hypnotised by the squeezing and sucking sounds, and the terrible sight that met her eyes.

Granny's garden dreams were being forced from her head. Flower after flower was extracted from her poor sleeping mind and poured into the monster's slack, waiting stomach. Its pale innards were filled with showers of exotic petals, shimmering leaves and round ripe fruits and soon it was fat with stolen colour.

"No!" Finch shouted. "Not Granny. Not my granny!"

She wielded Grandpa Field's walking stick above her head. But the creature, seeming satisfied with its catch came towards her, swam right round her and back out onto the landing. It made for the staircase, sliding away down the polished wooden banister. Finch careered after it, stumbling as she tried to go faster. It was crazy to chase a monster, but she was so furious she couldn't help it.

She almost caught up with it in the hall. She even forgot to be afraid and began snatching at it with her bare hands, but it was so slippery, she couldn't catch hold and it rose up out of reach.

"Stop!" She pursued it into the pantry, flicking on the light as she flew through the door. The little square window just below the ceiling was open as always. The creature didn't hesitate. It surged up over the shelves crammed with jars of raspberry jelly and rosehip jam, and eased itself out through the little window and out of the house.

With Philip staying close at her heels, Finch ran to the front door and hauled it open. There was no moon visible but the outside light was on. Its muffled yellow

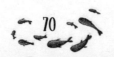

70

glow was enough for her to see the creature sail into the gloomy night and climb, like an overfed dolphin, through the grimy air. Up it went, swirling its way around the Empress, before disappearing. Straight into the cloud.

Finch stood, panting on the doorstep. Apart from her own breathing the night was utterly still again, as if the creature had never been there.

But Finch knew what she had seen.

The boy had not been lying. The cloud monster was real. Everything Tomas had said was true.

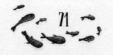

Nine

"Whatever was I thinking?"

Granny Field was still in her dressing gown, standing by the window in her bedroom, gazing out. It was midday.

"Granny?" Finch lingered in the doorway, holding a cup of tea. She had not gone back to bed that night. She had not been able to bring herself to go back up the stairs for fear of what she might find. She had curled up on the sofa and stayed there, huddled under a blanket with Philip, sleepless, waiting for morning.

And when morning came she had kept on waiting. She'd been hoping for Granny to come springing down

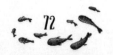

the stairs, hoping to hear her whooshing water into the kettle, clattering about in the kitchen as usual. Then Finch would know the cloud monster wasn't real at all, just an awful, horribly life-like nightmare.

But the kettle had stayed cold all morning and Granny Field had not appeared. Finch had finally summoned up the courage to go and find her, to see for herself.

"Whatever in the world was I thinking?"

"Thinking about what, Granny?" Finch's chest felt tight as she said it.

"That garden," Granny said. She was looking at it almost as if she'd never seen it before in her life. "Why did I take on such a big one? I can't manage a garden like that. Not at my age. I should sell up at once. Get rid of it."

Finch swallowed. "But you love the garden. Remember? It's your favourite thing in the whole world."

Her granny only shook her head. "Was, maybe." She turned and shuffled back to her bed.

After what she had seen in the night, Finch had almost been expecting something like this, but she was

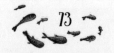

still very shocked. Granny Field had had bright white hair for as long as Finch could remember, but she had never seemed old at all, and she had certainly never behaved like a fragile old lady. But that was what she looked like today.

She wanted to fling herself onto the bed, hug Granny Field and tell her about the cloud monster so that they could decide what to do about it, but she couldn't somehow, not with Granny like this.

She perched instead on the very edge of the bed, putting the cup of tea on the bedside table, and laying down Grandpa Field's stick on the blanket. She had been keeping it by her side, just in case. Granny Field picked it up and stroked it absently.

"Ah, my Glen!" she murmured. "Never a cross word between us. Except that one time. But never again. Never again."

"What do you mean?" Finch said. She hated hearing her wonderful granny talking in this confusing way. She raised the cup of tea. "Aren't you coming to have breakfast? I've made you a cuppa, look."

"Not just now," Granny pulled the covers over her legs. "I've no get-up-and-go today, Finch. Will you be

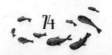

74

all right on your own for a little while?"

"If you like." Finch gulped back the sob that welled in her throat. Granny Field didn't seem to care about the tea, she didn't seem to care about Finch either. It didn't seem to bother her whether she stayed or not. She hardly even looked at her.

Finch groped blindly for the door, and went straight downstairs. She had lost her brilliant, confident granny, just like that, overnight, and she didn't know what to do. She couldn't call Mum and Dad to tell them about it because they were thousands of miles away, and anyway, how could she explain to them about a cloud monster that stole dreams? They'd say she was making things up.

Wandering restlessly from room to room, she picked up Granny Field's garden notebook and hugged it. She flicked her way to and fro through the pages, too distracted to look at them properly. But she stopped when she saw the page full of pond sketches. Each one was shaded in heavily, in grey. Each one was remarkably similar to the next. Each one had a date against it. There were ten of them in all.

"These aren't pond designs at all!" Finch said aloud.

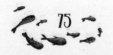

75

Suddenly she knew exactly what they were. They were sketches of the cloud, one for every day it had been in Sunview. Granny Field had been as worried about the cloud as everyone else. She must have been putting on a brave face for Finch's sake.

"I wish you hadn't done that!" Finch cried, with only the ticking of the kitchen clock to answer her.

Unable to bear the too-quiet house a moment longer, she rushed outside and went striding down the garden. Philip trotted after her and sat down next to her as she gazed over the grey, still town and the deserted beach below. Sunview-on-Sea had been stripped of its joy and its spirit, and Finch had never felt so alone.

She kept hoping Dave would arrive. She listened out for his van, but he didn't appear. *In any case*, she thought, *what use would Dave be now?* His dream had been snatched away, just like Granny's, just like everyone's. The cloud monster had ruined everyone in Sunview-on-Sea. The people of Sunview were Finch's only friends and the cloud monster had robbed her of them all.

She was the one person in the whole town whose dream was still intact, the one person who still knew

and remembered how things were supposed to be. She felt cheated and alone.

"Well then," she said aloud. "If that's the way it is, I'll just have to be the one to sort it out, won't I?"

The cloud above her looked enormous, like a vast railway station. It was so low in the sky now that Finch couldn't even see the topmost branches of The Empress. The tree must be poking right into the cloud.

And that, Finch realised, was the answer! She decided, right then. She would go to the cloud herself and confront the monster. She would make it give up the dreams and she would bring them back with her. "And you," she said to The Empress, "can be my ladder!"

The highest part of the tree looked very spindly, but Finch was nimble and light; she felt sure she could reach the top of it. She wasn't worried about that. The only question in her mind was, would the cloud actually hold a human being – even a small one? Most clouds wouldn't. They were nothing but vapour. This one was definitely more solid-looking than other clouds, but as to whether it would hold her – she would just have to find out.

77

She bent to undo Philip's lead. "Stay here, boy," she told him. She wished she could take him with her, but dogs couldn't climb trees and she was going to need both hands free if she was to manage it herself. "I'll be back soon."

The dog looked at her with doleful eyes.

"Take care of Granny Field, okay? That's your job. In you go now." She pointed to the open door of the house but Philip lay down with his head on his paws and whined. She felt like giving him a pat but she had to be stern.

"Inside!" she commanded. "Now!"

Philip went but his tail stayed down, pressed between his legs. He was doing his best to let her know that he thought she was making a mistake.

Maybe he was right. Finch had nothing with her — no tools or weapons, not even an outdoor coat. She wasn't prepared in any way. But how *did* you prepare to challenge a cloud monster? What weapons could you fight it with? She would have to make do with what she had. Her plan was flimsy to say the least, but a flimsy plan was better than no plan, and having it made her feel a little better.

Spitting on her palms to get a decent grip, she glanced back one more time at Hilltop House.

"I'll be back, Granny," she said. "I will. And I'll bring your dream back with me!" Then she took hold of The Empress's trunk, shimmied herself up it, and began to climb.

Ten

It was only when she was approaching the top of
The Empress that Finch began to waver. She had
clambered up swiftly and easily, not faltering for a
moment. She'd always been a good tree climber and
she wasn't afraid of heights. She'd once fallen out of
a tree when she was little; she had a dim memory of
floating to the ground and landing with a bump on her
bottom. Her mum had been in a dreadful panic when
she'd picked her up. She always said it was a miracle she
hadn't hurt herself, and that she must have bounced.
But Finch wasn't put off by the fall. She had gone on
climbing whenever she could.

Now, perching in the swaying branches, looking down over the roofs of the town, she suddenly found herself wanting to jump. She had an almost overwhelming desire to take off and fly, just like she did in her dream. She could let go of the tree now, and leap into the air. She imagined herself flying freely over the town. It would be so amazing; she longed to do it.

She leaned from the branch, arms stretched behind her, her chest pressed outwards so that she felt like a figurehead on the prow of a ship. How wonderful it would be to cut through the sky the way a boat cut through water. She could do it too. All she had to do was let go of the tree.

Her fingers were even beginning to loosen when a faint wailing sound reached her, sliding up on the air, and she recognised little Delia's voice. "Wa-want puddles!" she cried. "Want my we-wellies!"

Finch blinked hard and gripped the branch. She pulled herself back fast, and clung to the tree, gasping. What had she been thinking? Did she want to kill herself? The air must be thinner up here – it was making her light-headed. Of course she couldn't fly! Perhaps everyone at school was right, perhaps she

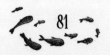

really did have feathers for brains. She shook her head and concentrated on the cloud. It was only a couple of metres above her head now. It was time to find out what it was like inside.

She climbed on, carefully negotiating the upper branches which bent beneath her weight, silently thanking each one for not giving way completely, until finally she reached the base of the cloud. It felt horrible – damp and dense to her touch.

"No going back now," she said.

She took a deep breath, closed her eyes and mouth tight, pressed her head against the cloud and pushed.

She tried not to panic, feeling as if a million clammy cobwebs were pressing on her face, her neck, her nose. The cloud was smothering her, blinding her. If it was like this all the way through she would never be able to see or do anything inside it, but she forced herself on, screwing up her face. A few moments later there was a wet popping sound, like a bubble bursting, and her head thrust through into an open space.

Finch rested for a second, breathing heavily. The thick spongy stuff she had squeezed through must only be the outer layer of the cloud, because now she was

in what looked like a large dome-shaped hall. The hall didn't seem to have any walls, or doors or ceilings. The edges of it were fuzzy and blurred and there were no visible corners, so it was hard to know where anything began or ended. Finch peered cautiously around. She couldn't see much, but she was all too aware that whatever was in here might be able to see her perfectly clearly.

As her eyes adjusted, she saw that she had emerged into almost the centre of the hall. Just ahead of her was a tall shape, almost as tall as The Empress. It was some sort of tower. Not a carefully constructed tower of stone or bricks, but a great jumble of things, piled haphazardly, one on top of another. It was all held together by what looked like fishing nets. Ropes stretched down and away from the tower, securing it to something – Finch couldn't see what.

It may have been pegged down, but the tower was still wobbling precariously. The objects caught in the nets moved and shifted about. Some of them seemed to be breathing, or perhaps sighing.

Growing more used to the gloom, Finch made out an open parasol, some broad palm leaves and a

coconut. There was a police helmet, a giant lollipop and a dangling doctor's stethoscope. A group of softly cooing doves huddled in the arched openings of a bright white dovecote. A shoal of large grey fish swam slowly about, while tiny orange fish flashed around them like darts. There was an oversized head of a smiling man wearing a crown, a daffodil perched jauntily behind his ear. There was a spinning globe with a map of the world. There was an iceberg with a polar bear on it, a desert and a coral reef. And there was a basket of tiny, sleeping kittens.

It was such a strange collection. Finch had never seen anything like it. Nothing seemed to go with anything else. None of it made much sense. But in amongst the assortment of objects Finch saw a few things she recognised. Polished black and yellow bowling balls rolled about, shining out at her. Next to them floated a copy of the *Sunview Gazette* with a picture of a trophy and a headline in thick bold print: *Fred takes gold at last*!

"Fred's dream!" she whispered, certain she was looking at Fred's dream of being a Crown Green Bowling Champion.

The objects in the net were stolen dreams!

The bowling balls were near the bottom of the pile, which made sense since Fred's dream must have been one of the first to be stolen. *Poor Fred*, Finch thought. *No wonder he'd let the bowling green go to seed.*

Fred's wasn't the only dream she recognised. The elaborately iced cakes and shiny, sticky buns revolving above the bowling balls must belong to Irena. That was why she had stopped baking and singing, and why the Conch Café now smelt only of cigarettes – because her dream of a bakery was up here and not in her head.

A pair of red wellington boots jumped about impatiently, as if they were trying to attract Finch's attention. It took her a few moments to realise that they must be Delia's dream. They explained why the little girl was so upset. All she wanted was to wear a pair of red wellies with yellow dots on them, and leap in some puddles. It was such a sweet wish of a dream. Who in the world would want to steal it?

The most recent thefts had already been spewed out onto the top of the pile. Dave's koala bear looked sorrowful as it tried to shelter under the rolling wave. It made Finch angry all over again to see it there. But the sight of the dream that lay above it made her angrier still.

At the very top of the tower was a spreading canopy of leaves, blossoms and water-lilies, and some huge, luscious-looking peaches – so ripe, their velvety skins were cracking and showing beads of amber juice. Granny Field's dream was so big and exuberant it made the entire tower of dreams look like a tree itself, blooming and fruiting all at once. Enormous flowers, dancing with butterflies, fluttered their petals against the netting. Fleshy leaves, in every shade of green, flapped and rustled indignantly. Tendrils of climbing plants curled themselves around their stringy prison.

Finch gritted her teeth. She would free Granny's dream. She would! She would free the other dreams too. All she had to do was pull the net off them, then she could push them one by one through the cloud and back into the branches of The Empress. True, some of them might have more difficulty getting down than others. The koala bear would be fine and the wellington boots looked as if they could walk by themselves. But cakes couldn't climb. How would they manage?

"I'll carry them." Finch whispered. She was so determined to return the dreams, she felt she could make a hundred trips if necessary.

She turned slowly and peered further into the hazy depths of the cloud hall, wondering if it was safe to put her plan into action. Now she noticed smoky corridors, five of them, stretching away from the hall like long sleeves she couldn't see down. Everything seemed very quiet. There was no sign of the monster. She shuddered at the thought of it; she never wanted to see the thing again. She pressed her palms together, willing herself on. She'd come this far. She had to keep going.

She was still only half in the cloud. She could feel her toes, hooked round the delicate uppermost branches of The Empress. Reaching out for one of the long ropes that tethered the dream tower, she took hold of it in both hands, and pulled herself fully up into the cloud.

Then, keeping one arm tightly round the rope, she tested the ground, gingerly putting down one foot at a time. Her feet disappeared into mist again but they found firm enough ground. Standing inside the cloud was like standing on damp sponge, but at least it held her weight.

Glancing down behind her, Finch saw that her body had made a sort of tunnel in the cloud. She could see

The Empress and the dull sky beneath, but the tunnel was already steaming over and the tree's topmost branches were fading into the mist. She would have to act quickly, before she lost her way out.

"Now or never, Finch!" she whispered.

Forcing herself to let go of the rope, she slipped forward as lightly as she could towards the tower of stolen dreams. She began searching for an edge in the netting that she could lift and pull. It was difficult, feeling around in the steamy atmosphere of the cloud. She wished she'd thought to bring Granny's kitchen scissors. Then she could have simply cut the dreams free.

At last she found a slacker section of netting. She was just beginning to work her fingers underneath it when something damp squelched beneath her toes. Worrying that she had trodden on somebody's precious dream that had somehow come loose, she reached down into the fog and picked up whatever it was, holding it up to her face so that she could see it properly.

Finch stifled a scream.

It wasn't one of the dreams. It was the cloud

monster. And she was holding one of its stalked
antennae in her hand.

Eleven

Finch let go instantly. She froze, horrified, sure the monster would spring up and attack her at any moment. The monster's sucking trunk was so strong, it could probably swallow someone her size whole if it wanted to. Her heart battered wildly against her chest as she waited to be pulled off her feet and sucked into oblivion.

Nothing happened. She waited but the monster stayed quiet. The steam shifted a little where she had dropped the monster's head and, daring to look down, she saw more of it. It was completely still, not poised to jump at all, but flopped loosely across the floor, like an exhausted animal.

The monster must be sleeping, and sleeping very soundly, Finch decided - it hadn't stirred even when she had picked it up. Before, it had writhed and snaked all over the place. Now it looked as lifeless and wrinkled as an old party balloon. There was no movement at all, not even the rhythmic rise and fall of breath.

Finch's hand felt clammy and greasy where she had touched it. She wiped it on her dress. If the monster was sleeping this deeply she had a good chance of freeing lots of the dreams – maybe even all of them – before it woke up. But she needed to get moving.

She set to work again, quickly finding the gap in the net. She was about to pull on it when, to her amazement, the entire net suddenly came right off the tower, apparently all by itself. It rippled down towards her and she had to step quickly backwards to avoid being caught in it herself. In her haste to get out of its way, she tripped over her own feet and fell silently to the cloudy floor. She stayed there, up to her shoulders in mist, watching the dreams drift about, as if they didn't realise they had been freed. Finch didn't know how they had come free, but she knew she hadn't done it.

She was about to get up when a voice, shouted,

"Dance! Dance, will you!"

A small ballerina Finch hadn't noticed before in the netting stood forward in mid-air, looking down sadly, her pretty little feet fanning outwards, heels together.

The voice came again. "Dance! Dance, I say!" It sounded crabby and irritable.

Reluctantly, the ballerina rose up on her satin pink toes, her tutu quivering around her. She didn't dance, but she looked forlorn and seemed afraid of whoever was speaking. Finch craned her neck to see who it could be.

"Why are you being so disobedient? Are you deaf?"

There was a great deal of tutting and sighing and then a man appeared, moving steadily around the tower of dreams. Finch hadn't heard any footsteps but the man must have come down one of the fog-filled corridors without her noticing. She couldn't see the whole of him even now, because of the mist that coiled and flowed about with him, but she could see he had blue hair and a long, tatty blue beard. He wore a big blue overcoat, too, with flapping tails, and he was holding a long stick. He flourished the stick as he went, flicking it about in the air, making the dreams wince and

92

jump as he passed.

"You!" he barked at one of Irena's cakes. "I command you, cut yourself open and give me a slice. Let me have a taste of you."

Nothing happened, except Finch thought the cake sank a little in the middle, as if it was sad to be addressed so rudely.

"Bah!" the man complained. "You great clod of crumbs! You're as bad as the rest of 'em." He moved on and pointed his stick at a pair of diving fins. "Swim!" he shouted. The fins crossed themselves, one over the other, as if for protection. The man didn't seem surprised. Finch thought he must have tried this before. "What's the matter with you all?" he demanded as he circled the dreams. "Why won't any of you perform? Why won't you do as I say? It's disobedience, that's what it is! Well I won't have it. This is your new home. You have a new master now. The sooner you get used to that fact, the better!"

In his annoyance he leaped up into the air and Finch saw with a shock that the man didn't have any legs. Instead, he had a blue and silver tail which he spread out in a flickering fan, just like a peacock's.

93

Finch put a hand to her mouth to stop herself from crying out as the man hovered above her, tail whirring.

He wasn't a man. He was half man, half bird!

Twelve

Still hovering in the air, the man-bird reached up with the stick, which Finch now saw had a metal hook on its end. He hooked it smartly under the koala bear's armpit and brought the bear down. He reminded Finch of a fairground stallholder she'd once seen, hooking down a cuddly toy for a prize. Only this man-bird wasn't as friendly, and he seemed to want the prize all for himself.

The koala bear squealed as it fell. The man-bird caught it and shook it.

"What use are you?" he said. "What use? A whinging ball of fluff!" Above him, Dave's kookaburra let out a

loud gargling sound. Finch knew it was the bird's alarm call but it sounded just like mocking laughter. The man must have thought it was taunting him, and he gave the koala another, even rougher shake. It cried out like a terrified baby.

"There you go again!" said the man-bird.

Finch was so outraged she didn't stop to think. She leapt up, waded over and hurled herself at the man.

"Let it go!" she shouted. She made a grab for the koala, but her hand closed on a clump of blue and silver tail feathers. "How can you be so cruel? You let it go!"

"What's this? What's this?" The man-bird spun round with the koala on his front, Finch clinging grimly to the end of his tail. He whirled round and round so fast she couldn't hold on. She flew off, propelled straight into the tower of dreams, and landed at its foot, rolling right into it, upending the kitten basket and scattering shoals of dream fish.

Now that he could see her, the man-bird seemed to lose all interest in the koala bear. He tossed it back up into the tower where it crouched down behind Delia's dream boots. *It would be safer there*, Finch thought. But as the man-bird rearranged his shimmering tail and

floated towards her, she began to see that revealing herself to him might not have been the wisest of moves.

For now he was paying extremely close attention to her.

"Who's this?" he barked. "A trespasser, is it? An unauthorised intruder? Come on, let's see you."

There was nowhere to run to. Finch kept very still. She didn't take her eyes off the man-bird, and as he came closer she saw the fierce expression on his face change to one of intense concentration.

"Well, well. What have we here? What indeed!" He touched her hair with his fingers. "The colour of morning light," he whispered. For a moment he seemed lost in thought, but then he threw back his head and laughed. "Oh, Serendipity!" he crowed. "Look what the wind blew in! Hee hee!" He patted Finch's hair again, as if she was a curious stray animal he'd found.

"Who are you?" she demanded, jerking her head away. Her heart was hammering but she refused to be afraid. "*What* are you? Are you working for the cloud monster? Is that it? Are you its servant?"

The man didn't seem to hear her. His head was still thrown back and his eyes were all scrunched up as he

went on laughing. "Perfect! Oh perfect!" he chortled.

"What's perfect?" Finch hadn't known what to expect in the cloud, what dangers or obstacles she would meet, but she certainly hadn't expected to be laughed at. "And I don't see what's so funny!"

The man wiped tears from his eyes and gasped for air.

"Of course you don't see," he managed to say at last in a shrill piping voice. "How could you? You don't know it, child, but you have just made an improvement to my master plan. A significant improvement. Oh, I've been working on this plan for years. Years I tell you. But I never came up with anything this good. Oh, this is marvellous!"

Finch was furious.

"Stop laughing!" she snapped, lurching to her feet. "Stop it, you evil . . . blue . . . bird beast!" She launched herself at him again, slamming her hands into his chest. "I don't know who or what you are, but I'm here for the dreams. I've come to take them back!"

The man-bird, still laughing his high pitched laugh, held onto her fingers and prevented himself from toppling over by beating his blue tail from side to side.

Finch struggled madly, but although the man-bird was small, hardly any taller than she was, his grip on her was tight and she couldn't free herself. Then suddenly, he dropped her to the floor.

"What a triumph this will be!" he said, opening and closing his astonishing tail. At least he'd stopped laughing, although he still seemed to be fizzing with excitement. "Why shouldn't I do it? Why shouldn't I? It will be the sweetest revenge." He scrunched his hands into fists and then clapped them together.

"What revenge?" Finch said. "What are you talking about? Revenge on who?"

"On the landleggers, of course."

"What are *landleggers*? And who are you? Are you that monster's servant?"

"Certainly not!" The man-bird looked very put out. "I am Maverick," he said haughtily. "I am a sky spirit."

"A what?" Finch had never heard of sky spirits.

"Yes. I, Maverick, am a sky spirit. And you may be sure I am nobody's servant. The monster, as you call it, serves me and not vice versa. The 'monster' is nothing but a puppet. *My* puppet." He dragged the lifeless body of the monster from the floor and then tossed it aside.

99

He tapped his chest with a blue thumbnail. "I am the only master here."

No wonder the monster seemed so different now. Finch had thought it was just sleeping, but it wasn't even alive. Her real enemy, she realised, was right in front of her. If she was going to fight him she needed to find out more about him.

"What are sky spirits? What do they do? Are there more like you?"

"Of course." The man-bird, Maverick, settled near her on the floor. "You would never see us, but we are here. We live among the clouds, in our allocated areas. And we scatter dream dust."

"Dream dust. What's that?"

"The dust that provides landleggers with their dreams, of course!" He slapped his tail shut, impatient at the interruption.

Then he swished it open again, frilling it out to its full extent as he went on. "Sky spirits are a noble race and they do important work. They are the givers and guardians of dreams." He sniffed. "But that's all in the past for me. Long past. And I," he announced proudly, "am the first sky spirit to work out how to take dreams

away again." He flicked the monster's limp trunk with his tail. "It's my own system, don't you know? It's taken me many years to perfect."

"But why?" Finch said. To be able to give people dreams must be so wonderful, she couldn't understand why anyone would want to take them away again.

Bewildered, she stared at Maverick, and he stared back at her.

He came closer, rubbing his long, wispy beard and smirking.

"But to think," he said ignoring her question, his hand hovering above her hair again so that fear prickled its way across her scalp, "to think that I was going to be content with mere dreams."

Thirteen

Flinching away from him, Finch heard rustling, tutting and murmuring coming from the dreams behind her. It was as if they were listening to Maverick's words, as if they understood and were disturbed by what they heard. Did he mean to keep her here, against her will?

"I don't know why you've done all this," she said, trying to be firm but feeling very uneasy. "But it isn't right. I've come to take back the dreams. You give them to me now and I'll return them to their real owners."

"Oh, listen!" crowed Maverick. "Rightful this, rightful that. You're very sure of what's right, aren't

you, young lady? So I should give them back, should I? And what, may I ask, do you propose I do after that?"

"And then you can go." Finch stood her ground. "And you can take your cloud with you."

Maverick flapped his hands impatiently. "Oh, no, no no! I can't do that. Not when I've done so much work and made such progress. I mean, look what I've achieved already." He reached down and pulled up a silver pipe, extending it upwards from the floor. He passed it to her, gesturing for her to look into it.

Uncertain about taking her eyes off Maverick even for a second, Finch looked.

She saw Middle Street magnified before her. All the shops were shut, with their blinds firmly down. The whole street was deserted.

Maverick nodded eagerly. "A good view, yes?"

It was. The silver pipe was a powerful telescope. So powerful, Finch could even see cigarette smoke floating through the air vent at the Conch Café. Moving the pipe around, she could see all over Sunview: the harbour, the bowling green, the beach, even the railway station. Every square metre, including Granny Field's garden. Finch checked but there was no sign of Granny

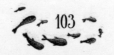

– just Philip, lying flat on the front step, ears cocked, waiting.

"Hold on, Philip," she told the dog silently. "I won't be long." She hoped it was true.

Maverick sneered. "Not much of a place nowadays is it? Not very *sunny* in Sunview-on-Sea? The landleggers are feeling the effects of my work at last. They're quite lost without their itty-bitty little landlegger dreams." He licked his lips. "But taking away one of their own kind and keeping her for myself – that's going to hurt, oh, so much more!"

A horrible chill spread through Finch's stomach as she realised that Maverick really was talking about kidnapping her.

"Why do you hate us so much?" she asked, trying to keep her voice steady.

Maverick tugged peevishly at the lapels of his coat. "I'm teaching someone a lesson. That's all you need to know."

"I don't understand you," Finch said. "But you can't keep me here. You can't just go around kidnapping people. It's against the law!"

Maverick widened his eyes. "What?" he protested. "I

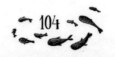

didn't kidnap you. You came here of your own accord. And as for the law!" he scoffed, "the laws of your land mean nothing to me. I'm not afraid of them. Because as you see," he spread his arms out wide and rose up a little, hovering above her, "I am quite literally *above* them!"

"You won't get away with it," Finch said. "I'll be missed. People will come looking for me."

"I doubt it." Maverick looked sly. "Think about it, my dear. Who knows you're here?"

Finch remembered with a pang that she hadn't told Granny Field or anyone else where she was going. Had Maverick been watching so closely that he knew that too?

"Philip!" she burst out. "Philip knows where I am!" She tried to sound confident.

"Philip?" Maverick raised an eyebrow. "Forgive me, but isn't he a dog? A landlegger pooch? A simple pet?"

Finch bit her lip. Maverick had been spying on the town so closely, he seemed to know everything about it.

"Yes, he's a dog. But he's a very clever one!"

Maverick smiled dismissively. "A mere dog can't help you now."

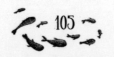

"Someone will come," Finch insisted. "They'll come and they'll rescue me!"

Maverick snorted. "Who? Not those dullards down below. No one down there has enough gumption to stage a rescue."

Finch thought of the state Granny and the others were in. They hardly had the energy to drag themselves out of bed in the mornings, let alone find their way up into a cloud. She was terribly worried that Maverick had a point. And now he was coming towards her, flicking the end of his tail purposefully as he approached.

She backed away. "What are you doing? Leave me alone!"

"That's right," Maverick said, wafting his blue-nailed hands at her. "Back, back you go now." He hustled her along towards the dreams. She searched around desperately for her tunnel – her escape route – but the mist was everywhere and she couldn't find it.

Maverick gave her a light push and she tumbled backwards. The dreams gathered around her as she fell, as if they would like to catch her, but couldn't, and she found herself back on the spongy floor of the cloud.

"Now, I have preparations to make," Maverick said.

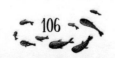

"I don't want you getting in the way, or slipping out of my sight somehow. And since, for some inexplicable reason, these ridiculous dreams are so precious to you, I think you should spend some time with them."

Finch saw the fishing net fly up and over the top of the dreams. It trickled downwards trapping them, and her, inside. Maverick pulled tight on the ropes, securing the net.

He put his hands on his hips and moved back to admire his handiwork. He stared up at the dream tower, taking it all in, all the way up to the spreading bloom-laden branches of Granny Field's garden dream. He nodded grimly, and with a satisfied swish of his tail he turned his back.

"Serendipity! Serendipity!" he chanted over and over again, as he went gliding away down one of the cloud's corridors. "Oh, my sweet Serendipity!"

He disappeared in a coil of mist, leaving Finch alone with the dreams.

She put out a hand to one of the kittens which had fallen from the basket and was gazing around sadly. It touched her palm with its tiny pink nose, then clambered up and flopped into her lap. She sat stroking

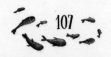

107

it, while the other dreams shuffled and murmured around her.

"Don't worry," she told the kitten. "I'll get you out of here. That man, that sky spirit or whatever he is, he won't have you in this prison for long. I'll make sure of that."

The outsized head, with the crown and the daffodil behind its ear, bobbed close to her. It had a very concerned expression on its face. It crossed Finch's mind that the face was a lot like Fred's face. Fred from the fish shop. Whoever had dreamed it, the face was kind and friendly, and she was glad of its presence.

"I'll do it, Prince Fred," she told it. "I will."

The face continued to smile but it looked doubtful too.

"You have to believe me!" Finch said. "I'll get you home. All of you. I'll get you back where you belong." But she didn't feel nearly as confident as she sounded. She'd been so rash, she hadn't thought it through. If only she had told someone where she was going! She hadn't made anything better. She'd made everything a thousand times worse.

"Feathers for Brains!" she hissed under her breath. She deserved that name more than ever now.

Fourteen

It was very warm and stuffy inside the net with the dreams all squashed in and clustered around her. Finch, exhausted from trying and failing to find an escape hole in the net, and from thinking as hard as she possibly could, had begun to feel sleepy. She was almost dozing off when she felt a sharp jab in her ribs.

"So this is where you have been hiding."

"Get away from me!" Finch jumped up, crossing her arms in front of her face, ready to attack.

"You don't have to be so . . . aggressive . . . you know," the voice panted. "Not when I've come all this way to see you."

Finch peered between her arms. A dark head was poking up through the cloud floor. "Were you even . . . going to send us . . . a postcard?"

"You!" Finch breathed.

Tomas smiled and hauled the rest of his skinny body up into the cloud, checking that the floor was going to hold him, just as Finch had done before. He was wheezing a bit, she noticed.

"Phew! That was quite a climb."

Finch let her arms drop. "Are you a dream? Am I dreaming you?" She had only ever dreamed her flying dream, but Tomas was so washed out and pale, he looked no more real than a ghost. Perhaps she really had fallen asleep.

"I don't believe I am a dream, in fact," Tomas wiped very real-looking sweat from his forehead. "But why don't you pinch yourself to make certain?"

Finch guessed he was teasing but she gave herself a slight pinch anyway.

It hurt.

"I'm still here, yes?"

"Yes," Finch said, then remembered Maverick and dropped her voice to a whisper. "Yes. But how did you

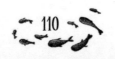

110

know *I* was here? Why have you come?"

"Monster hunters, remember?" Tomas said, following her lead and whispering too. "And it wasn't difficult to work out. I knew you must have discovered I was correct about the cloud monster. Aunt Irena told me where you lived, you see, and I came to your house to look for you, but no one was about except that little dog. He kept running to the big tree, and he looked so worried. I guessed you'd decided you could fix things all on your own. That would be just like you, I think."

Finch was about to say, "How would you know what I'm like?" but she stopped herself. This boy had climbed all the way up The Empress to find her, even though she had refused to believe his story. The day before, on the Camels, she'd shouted at him to shut up, but he'd been right then and he was right now. She *was* stubborn. She frowned in annoyance at herself.

But Tomas only smiled his crooked smile.

"So this is what people dream about." He gazed admiringly at the tower of dreams. "I wish I could do it. I like that big wave." He pointed at Dave's Australian surf. "And I see Aunt Irena's cakes are still here. Hey, that face with the crown looks exactly like the man in

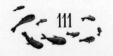

the fish shop!" He didn't seem scared by what he saw in the cloud, only fascinated.

"Where is the monster though? Why hasn't it eaten everything and destroyed it?"

Finch pointed to the hazy floor where the monster still lay.

"That's it?" Tomas said. "That bunch of soggy bath towels? It doesn't look very harmful now. Not very monsterish, is it?"

"No." Finch glanced around anxiously. It wasn't the cloud monster they needed to worry about now. Its controller was the real problem. She was suddenly very relieved to have someone to share that problem with.

"I'm so sorry I was mean to you before," she said. "I'm sorry I didn't believe you."

"You certainly didn't want to make a team with me. But I forgive you. Anyway, I'm used to it. No one ever wants to be in a team with me. I am always the . . . odd one. Is that how you say it?"

"The odd one out," Finch said. "Yes. I'm the odd one out, too. When we have to get into teams for PE I'm always last to be picked. I usually pretend I've

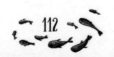

forgotten something and run back to the changing room so it isn't too obvious."

"I must try that too!" Tomas said with a smile.

Finch smiled back, embarrassed and a bit surprised by her own admission. Then, aware again of the extraordinary place in which they were having this ordinary conversation, she said, "Can you get us out of this net, do you think? Can you loosen those ropes?"

"I can try." Tomas followed the line of rope with his hands. "It's fixed to a hook here, it's actually hooked into the cloud. Clever! What an adventure this is!" He unhooked the rope and moved over to a second one. "How did you get yourself in there anyway? Are you going to tell me?"

"I will. I'll explain everything," she said, "but right now we need to climb back down The Empress. We need to get out of here fast." She lifted up the net where Tomas had loosened it. She was just about to crawl underneath it, when the kookaburra let out its loud clattering laugh.

Out of the corner of her eye, Finch glimpsed mist swirling towards them through one of the cloud corridors. They were too late. Maverick was coming

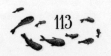

back. She didn't know what would happen if he found Tomas in the cloud, but she was quite sure it was nothing good.

"Quickly!" she hissed. "You have to hide!"

Fifteen

"I heard a commotion," said Maverick, sailing in. "What's going on?"

"Nothing," Finch answered at once. "I mean, I haven't seen anything."

"Haven't you, indeed." Maverick swished about suspiciously, checking over the dreams. "Well," he said, smiling at Finch all the while. "Well, well."

Seeming satisfied, he started to move away, as if to go back to his corridor. But just before he reached it, he stopped, pounced on one of the ropes Tomas had loosened and pulled it hard. He yanked off the whole net and rushed at the dreams, swiping at them and

rummaging through them like washing until, although the dreams did their best to cover him, Tomas was revealed at the bottom of the pile.

Finch couldn't help being impressed that Tomas didn't shout or scream, or try to run away as he had his first proper view of a sky spirit. He just stayed where he was on the floor, his eyes wide and dark in his pale face.

Maverick paused, tail feathers whirring. "I knew something was different. What's that doing here?" He poked Tomas with a blue fingernail. "I don't remember that."

"That's . . . he's . . . my dream!" Finch said, thinking quickly. Before Maverick could turn round she put a finger to her lips, warning Tomas not to speak. "I . . . fell asleep, you see. He . . . he must have slipped out of my head while I was sleeping.

"Oh yes," Maverick said, swimming round. "We didn't collect a dream from you before, did we, child? How careless." He came and settled behind her. "But tell me, why would you dream such a pale skinny little runt of a boy as that?"

If Maverick had insulted her like that, Finch

116

thought, she would have hit him on the nose, but Tomas didn't react. He stayed where he was, staring passively ahead, as if he couldn't even hear.

"Does there have to be a reason?" Finch said. "Don't dreams just come and go, in and out of your head, as they please?"

"No!" Maverick said. "Not these dreams. These dreams are all about wishes and hopes and desires. Every single one. That's why I brought them here. So you tell me, what would you want from that piffling stick of a feeble boy child?"

Finch frowned. Over Maverick's shoulder she saw Tomas mouthing at her.

"Friend," she repeated out loud.

"What's that?" Maverick almost growled.

"Friend," she said again. "I . . . want him to be my friend. Yes, that's it." It wasn't true, but it was as good an idea as any. The main thing was to prevent Maverick from realising Tomas was real. If he found that out, who knew what he might do to him?

"I want to make friends with a boy just like him," she went on. "I want a friend to play games with, because I'm lonely. I always have been. That's why I

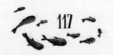

dreamed him. That's why the dream of him is here, to keep me company . . . I think."

She shut her mouth. She hadn't known she was going to say that part about being lonely. It had just slipped out with everything else. She hoped she hadn't overdone it. Maverick was very close to her, his nostrils twitching as if he was trying to sniff out lies.

Tomas took some small flat stones from his pocket, like the ones he'd been skimming that day at the beach. He began to play with them, setting the stones on the back of his hand, then flipping them off and catching them. He was pretending to be a dream, a dream of a boy you could play games with. It was clever of him, Finch thought. She admired how quickly he had understood what was going on up here. He hadn't made a fuss or screamed or anything. Tomas gave her a thumbs-up sign, then quickly put his hands behind his back as Maverick turned to him again.

"Is that it, now?" the sky spirit said, gliding backwards and forwards in front of Tomas and the other dreams. He seemed wound up, like an irritated wasp. "A dream boy. A dream boy friend. Is it indeed? Well I never." Maverick laughed his little high-pitched laugh as

118

if Finch had just told him a joke, but it didn't sound like real laughter.

"And you expect me to believe that!" he snapped, suddenly rounding on her. "What do you take me for, girl? A fool? Well, I'm not one. Far from it. I know exactly what dreams are here. I have catalogued them all carefully and there is nothing like this in my collection."

"No!" he shrieked, flying at Tomas. "I know a landlegger when I see one." He pulled Tomas to his feet by the neck of his jumper. "And what a pathetic specimen this one is. Why, I ought to throw you back out the way you came!"

He raised Tomas higher as if he was preparing to fling him from the cloud like a bag of rubbish.

"Stop!" Finch cried out, suddenly imagining Tomas falling helplessly all the way to the ground. "Please!"

Maverick stopped. "How touching," he said. "You really do care about the boy. Well, this may surprise you but I know what it's like to care for a companion. And why shouldn't you have one? Yes. It would be good for you to have someone of your own age along. We'll take him with us, shall we?"

He dropped Tomas right next to Finch so that their

elbows knocked together. "I was bringing you some supper, child, but now you can share it with your friend. There should be enough skymallows here." He drew a bag from inside his coat and handed it to Finch. It was full of blueish objects that resembled marshmallows.

"And it wouldn't be right to keep the two of you imprisoned in the dream net all night. I'm not that cruel. You can sleep here. This will be much more comfortable." He gestured towards some pillows on the floor, stuffed tight and stout as sandbags. Obediently Finch and Tomas went over and sat on them.

Maverick clapped his hands. "Good, good! Now, it's been a most exciting day, and I need my rest. We shall make more arrangements for the two of you in the morning." He began to drift back down his corridor. "I bid you good night."

As soon as Maverick disappeared Finch put a hand on Tomas's wrist. Close to the pillows, she had caught sight of black fingers pointing up through the cloud floor. She recognised them at once. The topmost branches of The Empress! If Maverick was going to leave them alone now, they might be able to escape after all. She stared at Tomas, then at the branches, and

back, silently passing the idea to him.

"However!"

They both jumped as Maverick's voice sliced through the air.

"We don't want any more of your kind finding their way up here, do we? Hoping to go on some sort of sky cruise. This isn't a pleasure boat, you know. And I'm not made of skymallows. So, just to be sure, we'll make a small adjustment to our position."

He stretched out his hands and raised them up slowly as if he was holding invisible strings. At the same time Finch felt the cloud move upwards like a lift and then settle again.

Maverick smiled and fluttered his hands at them. "Lie down now, landlegger children. Sleep, sleep!" He chuckled to himself as he whisked away.

As soon as she was sure he had really gone, Finch rushed over to where she had seen the twiggy branches. She checked and checked but there was nothing to see, and she knew The Empress was now far, far out of reach.

Defeated, she sank down next to Tomas on the pillows.

There was no escape.

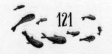

121

Sixteen

"It doesn't make sense, Finch. Why does he hate humans so much?"

They were sitting on their pillows, eating the tasteless skymallows. Night must have fallen some time ago but neither of them could rest, there was so much to think about. They could hear snoring coming from the other end of Maverick's preferred corridor, so they knew it was safe to talk out loud. For now.

"That's what I can't work out," Finch said, holding out the skymallow bag to Tomas. There was only one left. She was still hungry but he was so skinny, he looked as if he needed it more than she did. "I've told

you all I know about Maverick. He definitely wants revenge on someone."

"But on who? A human?"

"I don't know. He keeps saying this one word, though – Serendipity. I don't know what it means."

Their voices were so muffled in the dense atmosphere of the cloud, it was like speaking into a thick scarf and it made Finch feel very small. She let the last of her skymallow dissolve in her mouth and swallowed. "What time do you think it is now?"

"Not sure. Late, I think."

"Granny must be wondering where I am. Won't your aunt be worried too?"

Tomas shrugged. "I doubt it. I told her I was going to visit you, in fact. I said I might stay. But she is so gloomy, she hardly noticed me go."

Finch nodded. Everyone in Sunview was gloomy now. No one noticed anything much, thanks to Maverick. Angrily she screwed up the empty bag and jumped up. "We need to find out more about him. That way we'll know how to fight him."

"I agree," Tomas said, getting up too. "To know is to be powerful."

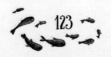

Finch looked at him. "You do say some odd things."

"It's because of all the books I've read," he answered. "I've spent more time reading books than talking to people. I don't talk to other children very much at all. I'm not good at conversation."

"I think you are," Finch said. "And I don't talk to other children much either. I usually prefer adults." Her adult friends didn't tease her, not like the children she knew at school.

"Ah!" Tomas gave a little nod. "Perhaps that is why the two of us get along so well, then. We hit it off immediately. No?"

Finch almost laughed. "No!" she said. They certainly hadn't got off to a good start but she didn't dislike Tomas any more. She was grateful to him for coming, and it was so much better having someone else to help work out what to do. She touched the frayed cuff of his jumper.

"I'm glad you're here."

"Yes," he smiled. "Now you don't have to be lonely."

"Oh, I didn't mean—" Finch began as Tomas led the way towards Maverick's corridor. "I just said that to Maverick to throw him off the scent."

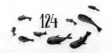

124

But of course Tomas was right, she really was lonely; she had simply been speaking the truth.

She caught up with him and they tiptoed down the corridor together, their feet bouncing silently across the floor of the cloud.

"You don't seem very scared," Finch whispered.

"I am," he whispered back huskily. "But I'm excited too. I like to be involved in a real adventure."

Finch nodded. "Did you do something very bad?"

"What? When?"

"Before. To be made to leave your school, I mean. And to come here. My granny said your parents sent you away."

"Oh!" Tomas chuckled. "That wasn't for being bad, although I wish it could have been. That would be so much more interesting than the truth. No, I was ill. I nearly died in fact. I was too ill to go to school all year, and now I have come to Sunview-on-Sea for the sea air. And the sunshine." he added wryly.

"Not much of that around," Finch whispered. She smiled at him and he smiled back. His dark eyes were thoughtful and kind. She wondered how she could have been so wrong about him.

 125

They fell silent. They were standing by a long curtain of cloud. Carefully, working together, they reached for a corner of it and pulled it upwards, folding it back on itself until they had just enough space to step into the misty chamber beyond.

They froze.

Maverick was watching them. He was perched on some sort of swing, his tail draped beneath him. He looked like a giant and colourful old hawk, ready to swoop down on its unsuspecting prey. Finch braced herself for the attack.

"It's okay," Tomas breathed after a moment. "He's still asleep."

Finch peered closer and saw that although Maverick's posture seemed alert, his eyes were closed and his shoulders moved gently up and down in time with his breathing.

They dared to move in a little further. There was nothing to see other than the same steamy vapour that filled the rest of the cloud. Maverick's chamber was empty. It held no clues at all. Not wanting to believe it, Finch and Tomas searched anyway. Going in opposite directions they padded softly round the circular room,

patting its curving walls, and meeting again all too soon.

Finch was so disappointed. "There's nothing here."

Just as she said it, she stepped on a mound in the floor, and almost stumbled. As she did so, a pouch fell open in front of her, right by her nose. The pouch was the size and shape of a pelican's bill, and it was fixed to the wall. Finch could see a book inside it. With a quick glance at Tomas, she plucked it from the pouch.

It was a large book with a creamy fabric cover. It looked handmade. A title was inscribed on the front in swirling letters:

Catalogue of Dreams
(collected and claimed)

Inside was a neat list of every dream in the tower, detailed in very fine, spidery handwriting. Each entry was accompanied by a delicately shaded drawing. It was a beautiful book, and the careful way it had been put together reminded Finch of something. She felt a pang as she realised it was just like Granny Field's garden notebook. It was upsetting to think that someone had put so much time and effort into something so horrible

— a whole catalogue of stolen property.

"How did you open this?" Tomas whispered, examining the pouch.

Finch nodded at the floor and the stud she had accidentally trodden on. It must have triggered some sort of mechanism.

Maverick was still sleeping soundly, air whistling in and out of his nose, so working fast, they both began searching for more of the floor studs. Tomas found one almost immediately. He pressed it, and a second pouch appeared. This one contained a series of hand-drawn maps, with a map of Sunview-on-Sea at the very front.

Finch tried another stud. This time a much larger pouch fell open. She gasped when she saw what was inside. Until now everything they had found had been cream or white or grey, blending in with the interior of the cloud, but here was a splash of vibrant red and gold. Finch pulled at the soft, glowing material. It crackled in her fingers. She pulled and pulled until she had armfuls of the stuff.

"What is it?"

Finch shook her head. "Don't know."

When the material was finally all out of the pouch,

Tomas took one end of it, Finch took the other, and they stretched it out between them until it was quite clear what it was.

A tail.

A tail as big as Maverick's blue and silver one, but even more glorious. A mass of soft and sparkling quills. It was so lovely, Finch couldn't help wrapping herself up in it, as if it was a sarong or sari. It felt magically silky and light. Tomas pulled some papers from the very bottom of the pouch. He flicked through them, then held one up for Finch to see. It was a drawing of a boy and a girl, both with fine long tails.

"Young sky spirits," Finch murmured. The boy spirit had blue hair, like Maverick's but brighter. The girl's fluffy hair was a bold poppy red.

"She looks like you," Tomas whispered. Finch shook her head as she took the picture from him. Surely it was only the fact that she was draped in a tail like the one in the picture that suggested the resemblance. But looking closer she couldn't deny there was something in the girl's narrow face and nose that reminded her of herself. "Who do you think she is?" she whispered.

A huge wail answered her.

129

"Serendipity! Serendipity!"

Finch dropped the drawing. Maverick was awake.

He swooped from his perch so fiercely and at such speed, Finch thought he was going to hit her, but all he did was clutch at the edges of the shimmering tail that clothed her, repeating, "Ah, Serendipity! My own sweet sweet Seren!" Finch was amazed to see he was crying. "Take it back, I beg you. Take it back. For pity's sake, take it back!"

"What is it?" she said. "What's wrong?" Did he want her to keep the tail on or take it off? Maverick seemed lost in his thoughts, almost as if he was dreaming.

"'I'll only go for a day, Maverick,'" he said in a light, sing-song voice. "That's what she told me. 'I'll come straight back.'"

"Who said? Go where?" Finch asked. He wasn't making sense.

Maverick's beady eyes brushed over her, barely seeming to see her.

"I warned her. I told her she could die. 'You don't know what might happen to you. It's never been done before.' Sky spirits knew the earth all right, but none of them had ever touched it. It was a terrible risk. But

she wouldn't listen to me. She was too fascinated. Wanted to know what earth was like for the landleggers. Serendipity was always far too curious for her own good. And for mine. It shouldn't have happened the way it did. We should have been roaming the skies together. If it wasn't for her stubborn ways we could have been doing that for the last forty years. Even now we could be happy." He crushed the tail to him. "She and I did everything together. Explored the skies. The heights belonged to the two of us. We were . . ."

He fell silent and clamped his arms around his stomach as if he was in pain again. Finch felt sure he had been about to say "in love".

"But what happened to her?" she said. "Where is Serendipity now?" From the way Maverick spoke, Finch wondered if she had died.

"Don't you know?" Maverick shot a fierce glance at her. "Isn't it obvious?"

He picked up the drawing and thrust it at her, his finger stabbing at the face of the girl sky spirit, scratching at her crimson hair. "Look again, child!" he said. "Look there! Don't you recognise your own grandmother when you see her?"

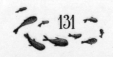

Seventeen

"My . . . what?" Finch's hands flew to her mouth as she stared at the drawing. "That's . . . my granny?"

"Yes," Maverick said, his voice tense and bitter. "It is. You landleggers all know her as Serena Field, but to me she will always be Serendipity."

No one spoke. A haze of mist wafted around them all.

"I should have known she'd leave me." Maverick dug his blue fingernails into the paper he held, as if he'd like to scrunch it into a ball but could not quite bring himself to. "Even back then. She was so curious,

132

so flighty. I should have seen the signs."

"Granny Field. A sky spirit," Finch hardly breathed the words.

"Yes, she was a sky spirit. Once. And she was everything to me," Maverick said gruffly. "Everything. But I was never enough for her. Oh no. She always wanted to know what else was out there. And then, one day, she flew right down to earth. That's not even legal, you realise. It's against the Sky Law."

Now that Maverick had started talking, telling his story, it seemed to bubble and gush out of him, like water spouting from a burst main. He was so involved with his memory that he forgot to bluster and swagger as usual. He looked younger and more innocent, lost almost, so that Finch could see in his face the young boy he must once have been.

"I followed her as far as I dared," he said, his eyes seeming to seek for something far in the distance. "Sky spirits aren't supposed to risk showing themselves to the landleggers; it's dangerous to go too close. I stayed back. I was more dutiful in those days. I stayed on the lowest thermal I could find, along with the birds. But she . . . she kept going. And she didn't

know how to land. She didn't know what ground was like, hadn't the first idea. How could she know?" His eyes watered with the memory. "The earth was so hard, no spring, no bounce. She hit it with such a thud. I'll never forget that sickening sound. And she went so still I was sure, sure she was dead!"

He put his head in his hands and tugged at his hair in anguish.

"But she wasn't dead," Finch prompted. She was desperate for him to go on with the story.

Maverick looked directly at her, but Finch could tell he didn't see her. He only saw what was stamped for ever in his memory.

"She lay so still in that meadow. Her lovely shape sinking in the flattened grass and flowers. I was going to go to her. I *was*," he insisted, as if they might not believe him. "I would never have left her behind. But then," he narrowed his eyes, "*he* came!"

"Who's 'he'?" Tomas said.

"That dullard, that clod-hopping fool with his great big muddy boots, and his face like a speckled hen!" Maverick grimaced with sheer distaste.

Finch knew at once he was talking about Grandpa

Field. He had had lots of freckles. Finch's dad had them too.

"He had to find her in the grass, didn't he? Nearly trod on her too, the oaf! And she had to wake. She woke just in time to see him holding out his dirty paw. And she looked at him with this dazed expression on her face. I tried to call to her. 'Seren!' I said, 'My Seren!' But she didn't hear me. She was only looking at him. At his ugly hand. And she took it. She took it and let that great thug pull her up. And when she sat up, her hair, her beautiful hair . . ." He ran his hands through the air as if he was stroking a woman's real hair. "It wasn't red any longer, it was pure white. And what did she have when she rose from the grass?"

"Legs," whispered Finch. What she was hearing was completely unbelievable, and yet it all made a strange sort of sense too.

"Legs!" Maverick hissed. "Yes. She was landed, and all I could do was watch. I watched her walk away with a pair of stupid wobbling landlegger legs and not a thought in her head for me. She didn't look back, you know. Not even once."

Finch was in a daze. She remembered Granny Field

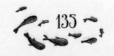

telling her how she and Grandpa Field had first met in the meadow above the town, amongst the cowslips and bee orchids. She fell in love with him and flowers all at the same time, she said. Finch knew it was then that Granny Field had begun to love plants. She didn't know it was also when she'd begun being a human.

Maverick snarled suddenly, shaking off the trance-like hold of his memory. "She forgot me!" he raged. "She never loved me, that's why. She didn't give two hoots. She only cared about the lumbering landlegger!"

"Perhaps she *couldn't* remember you," Tomas said thoughtfully. "She may have hit her head when she fell. That might be why her hair changed colour too, from red to white. It was the shock. I've read about that happening to people. They have a car crash or a bad accident and their hair turns to white at once."

"Don't go making excuses for Serendipity," Maverick said, swimming up into the air again with the end of the tail in his hands. He began unfurling it from Finch. "She simply didn't care," he said, spinning Finch round as he unwrapped her. "I was part of her old life. She forgot all about me, discarded me, just as she discarded this."

Finch stared at the tail slipping away from her. She

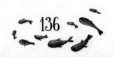

couldn't believe she had been touching Granny Field's own tail. She put her face closer to the last frilled feathers and thought she breathed in just the faintest scent of Granny Field.

Maverick snatched the end of the tail back, as if he couldn't bear for anyone else to share even the smell of the thing. "This lifeless scrap is all I have of her now," he said, pouring it back into its pouch in the wall. "I risked my own life picking it up. If I'd touched the earth or anything growing out of it, I would have been landed too. An imbecile landlegger just like her. But I didn't want that. I only wanted her. And when I saw she wasn't coming back, I wanted revenge. Revenge on her and all who are like her."

"And so you made your monster?" Tomas fixed Maverick with his calm gaze. He was still trying to make sense out of Maverick's ranting. "You made it to take away people's dreams."

"I did."

"But this all happened so long ago," Finch said. "Why now?"

"Because I'm ready. This is how long it's taken me to perfect my machine. I took myself away to a dark corner

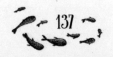

137

of the sky and I worked and I worked. I meant to crush
her. I would have crushed him too but I was too slow.
By the time I came back so many years had passed, the
landlegger – Field – was already dead. I wasn't going to
let that stop me though. I vowed I'd do it anyway. I'd
drain away her dreams, her aspirations, and those of all
her friends. And now I've done it!"

"But it's not fair!" Finch almost shouted. "Tomas is
right. I bet Granny Field didn't mean to hurt you. She
wouldn't hurt anyone. And the people of Sunview-on-
Sea don't even know about you. You're making them
suffer because of your old grudge."

"Too bad!" Maverick spat. He swam once round
in a circle. "I'll still have my satisfaction. But I never
thought," his said, his eyes lighting on Finch, "that
I'd have you too. Her very own grandchild. Ha! I may
have lost Serendipity to Earth and the landleggers.
But Serendipity and the landleggers have lost you to
me. That's what I call fair. A girl for a girl. That's true
justice, that is. Now they've lost you to me for ever!"

He was so excited he seemed to find new energy,
somersaulting in the air in front of them.

"What about forgetting and forgiving," Tomas said as

Maverick seized hold of their hands. "Why can't you let bygones be bygones?"

"Because they're not bygones to me!" Maverick bellowed, dragging them back down the corridor. "I still feel it right here," he used Tomas's hand to punch at his own chest, "just as I did on that first day. Why do you think I've kept these drawings – that tail – all these years? She meant everything to me! One minute she was with me, the next she was gone and I couldn't share anything with her any more – not the joy of flying under a double rainbow, not a joke, not so much as a bag of sky mallows! No. I could never see or speak to her ever again. My happiness was snatched away from me." He whirled them into the hall and let go of their hands so that they crashed to the floor. "And I want her to know just how that feels."

Watching him seething in the air above her, Finch finally understood exactly why Maverick's plan to keep her in the cloud had seemed so perfect to him. As she staggered to her feet she started to shiver, but not with fear. With fury.

"Granny Field may have hurt you," she told him, "but you're hurting so many innocent people. And even if

you keep me, you can't keep Tomas. Think of his aunt. What's she going to think when she finds he's gone? How is she going to feel? You have to let Tomas go. None of this has anything to do with him."

"That's his look-out!" Maverick huffed. "I didn't bring him here. I didn't ask him to come. Now that he's here, he'll have to stay."

"How will we live, though, Maverick?" Tomas stood up slowly, a puzzled expression on his face.

"What? What do you mean?"

"Well," Tomas began to pace about, interlinking his fingers, as if he was a young professor wrestling with a theory. "Finch and I will need good food, of course. Nutrition. We're still growing you see, and we can't live on a diet of sky mallows. We'll also need new clothes and showers, and haircuts. And there's our education to consider. Who will teach us things, give us lessons? Are you experienced in bringing up children?"

"Never mind all that!" Maverick squawked, startling the dreams which bobbed helplessly in their prison. "That's not the point. The point is I have been wronged, severely wronged, and you must all take the consequences!" He flew at them, beating the air with his tail.

140

"But Mr Maverick—" Tomas began.

"Stop trying to bamboozle me! I won't have it. Lie down, the pair of you, and be good." Obviously rattled, he pointed to the pillows he'd laid out for them before. "I need to clear my mind. I'm not used to all this squeebling and squabbling. It's giving me a headache. I'm going out for a fly."

With that he folded his tail, made himself go very straight, and spun round and round until he was going so fast he blurred, like an old fashioned spinning top. Still spinning, he began to descend, drilling a hole in the cloud floor with his body. He slipped away bit by bit, vanishing into the darkness.

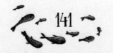

Eighteen

"What do you think his heart looks like?" Tomas said. "If he has one, that is." He was sitting on the pillows, picking at a hole in one of them, pulling out yellowish powder and sifting it through his fingers.

"Like a walnut," Finch answered. She leaned over the hole that Maverick had made and peered out at the dark sky. Sunview was somewhere below them, cloaked in deepest night. It made her own heart ache to think of Granny Field down there, and Philip – perhaps the only living soul who was worried about her, wondering where she was.

"Maverick's heart is like a walnut," she said again.

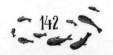

"Small, wrinkled and hard."

"You're right," Tomas nodded. "And his brain is a mouldy cheese with a million holes."

Finch couldn't help smiling at the idea. Tomas's strange thoughts were oddly cheering. Without him she would be in despair by now.

"Yes," she agreed, sitting down next to him. "Whatever Maverick's brain was like before, it's gone truly rotten now." She hugged her knees and watched the dreams floating in their tower.

"Why don't you have dreams?" she asked. "Is it really because you don't sleep enough?"

"Partly that," Tomas said, nibbling at an already non-existent fingernail. "But because I was so ill, I didn't think I had a future to dream about. Maybe that's why I couldn't do it. Because I had zero hopes and zero wishes."

That sounded so awful, Finch couldn't imagine it. "But you're better now," she said.

"Mostly. The doctors say if things go well I can make a full recovery. By the way, Finch," he added. "You didn't ever lose your dream, did you?"

Finch looked at him. "How do you know?"

 143

"Because you are still full of hope, still trying. Also, I've been looking," he nodded towards the heaped-up dreams, "and I don't think *your* dream is in there."

"No. You're right," Finch said. "I still have it. I've always had it. It's a flying dream. In my dream I can fly as well as any bird."

She was surprised to hear herself telling Tomas this. She had always promised herself she wouldn't tell anyone her dream again. She'd done it before and had been made to feel so stupid. But telling Tomas now felt natural, as easy as telling him what games she liked to play, or what her favourite meal was.

"Don't tell Maverick, will you?" she said. "If he finds out I've still got my dream, he'll make his monster take it from me. I'm sure of it. I'll have to stay awake so he can't."

The thought of having to stay awake made Finch suddenly feel extremely tired. She hadn't slept much at all the previous night and now they were well into the next. So much had happened in that time, she was exhausted.

"Don't worry, I won't tell that old fool anything." Tomas said. "And if you do fall asleep I'll keep watch."

144

Finch smiled gratefully and they both lapsed into silence.

How strange it was, Finch thought. Only days before, she had felt irritated and awkward in Tomas's presence, but now she was so relaxed in his company she could even have rested her head on his shoulder, if it wasn't such a bony one.

"Perhaps you really can, though," Tomas said after a while.

"Can what?"

"Fly."

"What?" Finch spluttered.

"I mean it. Perhaps you really can fly. You are one quarter sky spirit, after all. So." He spoke in such a matter-of-fact way, she knew he wasn't teasing her. He really meant it.

"I can't," she said, shaking her head. "I've never, no one can . . . it's just a dream."

"You say that, but look at all those dreams up there."

Finch did look and the dreams gazed mournfully back at her. Even the ones without faces seemed sad.

"I've been thinking about them," Tomas said, "while we've been in here. I've been thinking that they're all

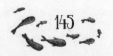

things that might really happen. They're wishes and ambitions, aren't they? Maverick said so. They're not just random dreams."

Finch studied the dreams. Delia's boots and Fred's bowling trophy weren't random. Nor was Dave's surfing dream of Bondi Beach, or the dream catch of fish that must belong to one of the local fishermen. They were all things people wanted to have, things they hoped to do. Things they had a chance of doing.

"Aunt Irena really would make a bakery at the Conch Café if she still had her dream cakes in her head," Tomas said, watching a large sponge cake revolving slowly in the air.

Finch nodded. "And Granny Field would make an exotic garden like the one at the top of the tower."

"So doesn't it follow," Tomas spoke quickly, becoming excited, "that you – you with your dream still in your head – doesn't it follow that you could carry it out? Really do whatever it is you do in your dream?"

"You mean, I could actually fly?"

"Exactly! Like a bird."

Finch shook her head. "But it's silly. I don't have wings. I don't have a tail!"

"Do you have either of those in your flying dream?"

"Well, no, but—"

"So maybe you don't need them. Maybe you are built like a girl, but maybe you can also fly like a bird."

Bird Girl! Bird Girl! The taunting words of Finch's school mates came back to her. Had they been speaking more truth than they knew? More than she knew herself?

"And," she swallowed nervously, "and you think I should try?"

"I'm just saying that logically it's a possibility."

It was odd to hear Tomas talking about logic. Nothing that had happened in Sunview-on-Sea this summer had been the slightest bit logical. But since her arrival in the cloud, things Finch had never understood before were fitting together in her mind. Her dream made her feel different because she really was different. She was part human, part sky spirit. Her dad took after Grandpa Field – everyone always said so – but she took after her granny. Granny Field's sky spirit genes had somehow passed through Dad, to her. That was why she had pale pink hair and why she dreamed of flying all the time.

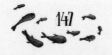

She turned to Tomas. "I fell out of a tree once, when I was small. I fell a long way and everyone made a giant fuss, but I didn't hurt myself at all. My mum said it was like a miracle."

"There you are then."

Yes. It explained everything!

"Your eyes are shining," Tomas said.

Finch almost laughed. "Are they?" Suddenly she felt more clear-headed and more alive than she had in her whole life.

And she thought, *why shouldn't I do it? Why shouldn't I try?*

Nineteen

Without stopping to think about it further, Finch jumped to her feet, took a little run and vaulted into the air. She ran forward but came down almost at once.

She leaped up again, managing a few more steps this time, flapping her arms wildly, but still she came down.

When it happened a third time, she stumbled and twisted her ankle hard. She cried out in frustration. "No. This is stupid. It's not working!"

"It nearly did," Tomas said, watching intently from the pillows, his chin resting on his knobbly knees. "Don't give up. Maybe you're trying too hard. How

does it work in the dream? Do it like that."

Finch thought. She never ran in the dream, only twisted in the air, making slight adjustments, her arms and legs stretched out behind her. Maybe Tomas was right, she was making too much effort. If flying was really natural to her, she needed to let it happen naturally, too.

"Okay. I'll try again."

This time, instead of rushing forward like a sprinter, she took a few slow steps. She closed her eyes and tried just to think herself into the air. She felt lighter at once. The damp atmosphere of the cloud seemed to flow over her arms. But she still wasn't moving. She wasn't flying.

At least she didn't think she was, until she heard Tomas cry, "Yes! You're doing it, Finch! You're really doing it!"

Finch opened her eyes. To her amazement she was at the very top of the cloud. She was airborne and about to fly straight into Granny Field's garden dream. Resisting the urge to put out her hands to save herself, she kept them back and instead turned her chest sideways. At once she veered away, easily avoiding a collision, and went weaving in and out of the trembling

150

blossoms and leaves. Gasping at her new skill, she flicked her feet and went faster until she was flying swiftly and smoothly, round and round the cloud hall, round and round the dreams.

It wasn't a lie and it wasn't a joke. She was really flying! And flying felt wonderful. It made her feel so different. It made her feel buoyant and strong, and more alive than she'd ever felt in her life.

"Look at me! Tomas! Look at me!"

It was like the time her dad first let go of the seat of her bike and she'd ridden it all by herself. It was like that, but a hundred, a thousand, a million times better. She felt so light and free, she felt as if she could do anything. Laughing, Finch pulled in her head and somersaulted right over. Then she did it again, and again, rolling over and over, just because she could.

She stretched her body out straight, then spun round and round until she was going so fast she knew she must only be a blur to Tomas. She came out of the spin and waved down to him, treading air as easily as if it was water in the swimming pool. Then, unable to resist, she shot off again, gliding, swooping, soaring. She was as high as the top of a double decker bus and

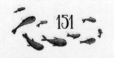

yet she wasn't scared at all. She was a diver, a gymnast, a kite with no strings to hold it. She didn't have wings but she was flying. She really was. She was flying exactly like a bird.

"Go, Bird Girl, go!" Tomas whooped and clapped from his place on the torn pillows. Finch laughed. Bird Girl was what the others called her when they wanted to mock her, but Tomas wasn't mocking her at all. He was cheering her on.

The dreams, too, did what they could to show their approval. The Prince Fred head smiled and nodded. Delia's little boots jumped up and down, Irena's cakes twirled and the kittens purred for all they were worth.

Now that Finch was up and flying she never wanted to stop, but she knew she must. She circled the dreams one last time and then flitted downwards, alighting next to Tomas, her toes curled over the edge of the pillows.

"I did it," she said breathlessly. "I did it! I really am a bird girl!"

"You are! You were brilliant!" Tomas flung his arms around her and she felt his bony ribs. Then he pulled away, coughing.

"Are you okay?" she asked, suddenly concerned as

the coughing seemed to take him over.

"Yes," he spluttered, struggling for breath. "Fine. I will be . . . fine . . . in a minute."

Finch waited for him to recover.

"I'm going to get you out of here you know, Tomas," she said, once the coughing fit subsided. "I'm going to make Maverick see sense. I think I know how, too. Granny Field. She's the way. If anyone can get through to what's left of his heart, it's her. He won't come to earth, though, so I'm going to have to bring her here."

"How though?" Tomas spoke croakily. "You can't carry her on your back."

"No," Finch agreed. That would never work. She'd only just learned to fly, she couldn't carry a grown person all the way up here, not even one as small and slight as Granny Field. "I'm going to do something better than that. I'm going to give her back her tail."

"You're going to steal the tail from Maverick?"

"It's not stealing," Finch said, taking off again. "How can it be? When I'm just returning it to its rightful owner?"

She flew down the corridor and yanked back the curtain to Maverick's chamber. She perched for a

moment on his swing, then dived down, looking for the studs in the hazy floor. Finding the one she wanted, she pressed it quickly. The pelican pouch opened once again and Finch hauled out the magnificent tail and flew with it back to the hall.

"Will you be all right here on your own for a little while?" She wrapped the tail around herself, knotting it securely around her waist. "I'll be back as soon as I can."

"Yes," Tomas said hesitantly, as he watched her. "I'll be all right, of course. But Finch, are you sure? Are you really going to fly outside in the sky? Are you sure you can do that?"

Finch leaned over the dark hole left by Maverick. Flying inside the cloud had been one thing, but flying in the real sky where there were winds and air thermals she'd never come across before would be another.

"Yes," she said, not letting herself think too hard about it. "Quite sure. And I'll be back for you, Tomas. I promise I'll be back. You came to find me, and I'll come back to find you, too."

Tomas was about to speak but she put up a hand.

"There's no time to argue about it. He could be back at any moment." She didn't look at Tomas. She knew

there was concern on his face and that it would spread to her if she lingered for another minute.

Before any more doubts could creep into her mind, she took three quick strides towards the hole, jumped up as high as she could, then dived down and threw herself headlong into the night.

Twenty

"No! Oh, no!"

Finch was falling. She fell through the cold night air, and she kept on falling. She was on her back, helpless as a beetle, unable to right itself. She might as well have jumped from a plane without a parachute. She'd made a terrible mistake. Everything she'd learned about flying just moments before was already forgotten and she was gaining speed with every second. If she carried on like this she would hit the ground like a missile. She would never survive the landing.

Helpless, she stared upwards at the base of Maverick's cloud and thought how that dreary grey was

the last colour she would ever, ever see.

Then, suddenly, a flash of silver.

At first she thought it was the pressure playing tricks on her eyes, but the silvery shape carried on moving across her field of vision and she realised she was looking at Maverick, shooting through the sky like an arrow, back towards the cloud. What would he do when he found she was missing?

What would he do to Tomas?

"Tomas," she murmured, as she remembered her promise to save him.

With a huge effort she pulled back her arms, swung up her legs and rolled, somersaulting forwards. She was still falling, but head first now, slicing through the air, hurtling towards the earth even more quickly than before.

"No," she said through gritted teeth. "Fly! I have to fly!" She struggled, striking out with her arms and legs, scrabbling at the sky, desperate to gain control.

"I can do it!" she willed herself on. "I can!"

And then, all at once, her upper body rose up, she felt herself level out, and she was lying on her front, back on an even keel. She really could do this. She

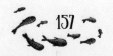

might not have a tail like true sky spirits, but her limbs did the work for her. She was swimming through the air. She leaped forwards, legs pressed tightly together, a dolphin in a sea of night. She tipped down again, not helplessly this time, but with new purpose and control.

It wasn't long before she heard the gentle swish of the sea on the sand. Then, despite the darkness, she could see the shapes of the town roofs. She could make out the bowling green pavilion, the spire of the church, the station clock. She had drifted off course a little but now she could pinpoint her position exactly.

She soared over the Three Camels, then dipped down close to the shadowy cliff face. Hovering for a moment above the beach, she sailed on, right over Middle Street, up through the town. The town where she knew everyone slept, still and silent and without a single dream to share between them. Finch struck out harder. There was no time to spare. She didn't follow the lanes with their twists and turnings, but instead made a beeline for the house at the top of the town, the one with the tallest tree that stood in front of it, upright and solemn as a sentry.

As she flew over the lawn Finch caught a whiff of

perfume. The creamy-white flowers of Granny Field's sea kale and night-scented stocks shone up at her, lining her route like tiny runway lights. Granny's window was directly ahead, and wide open. She flew straight for it.

It wasn't the most elegant of arrivals. Finch hadn't had much landing practice. She must have approached too fast because she rocketed through the window, grazing her shins on the sill, and then landing in a crumpled heap on the bed.

"Granny Field! Oh Granny!" Finch hauled back the duvet. "Wake up, Granny. I've so much to tell you!"

The bed was empty, the sheet smooth and cold.

"Where are you?" It was the middle of the night still. Granny ought to be here. Where else could she be? Finch was confused. She felt dizzy and disoriented from her flight. The room seemed to roll around her as if she was seasick. She hugged the covers and when the spinning still didn't stop she lay down flat to make it go away. She lay right in the middle of the bed, in the spot where Granny Field always slept, and let out a huge sigh. She knew she ought to get out of the bed at once and go looking for Granny Field but she was suddenly overwhelmed by tiredness. The bed was so soft, and the

duvet so puffy and welcoming.

She didn't mean to let her eyes close – it was the last thing she wanted – but her eyelids were so heavy they did it anyway, and she fell asleep.

Twenty-One

She was woken by a shrill barking and then Philip was charging in from the landing and leaping onto her chest, licking her face.

"Finch, love," Granny Field was there too, stroking her forehead. "Finch. I thought I'd lost you!"

Finch sat up in a panic. "How long have I been asleep?"

"Not long at all," Granny Field was fully dressed for some reason and holding onto Grandpa Field's gnarled old walking stick. "I was out in the garden when you came. I saw you arrive and we came straight up."

Finch realised Granny Field meant she had seen

her flying in through the window. Granny spoke quite calmly; she seemed to have taken the whole thing in her stride, but Finch was shaking uncontrollably.

Granny Field reached for her and hugged her. "Oh, my darling girl!" she said. "Hush, hush, you're safe now." She examined Finch's face. "Did he hurt you? What's he done to you? It is him, isn't it? Maverick. He's the one behind all this?"

"Yes, it's him," Finch's voice trembled as her granny inspected her for cuts or bruises. "He didn't hurt me, but he wanted to kidnap me and he's got Tomas!"

"Irena's Tomas?" Granny's face darkened.

"Yes. He came to find me, you see. He's still up there in the cloud, with all the dreams. Maverick's stolen the whole town's dreams. Yours too."

Granny Field pursed her lips, her mouth set in a thin straight line.

"You knew, didn't you, Granny? You knew all along it was him."

"I didn't want to believe it, but the minute I saw that cloud come over us, somehow I just knew." Granny sighed. "I blame myself Finch. I should have known something like this would happen one day. If you

162

leave loose ends they have a terrible habit of getting themselves in knots you can't easily untangle. But I never could have guessed Mav would do this. Is it really all because of me?"

"Yes, I think so."

Pressing her hands against her cheeks, Granny Field shook her head. "It's all so long ago!" She turned her attention back to Finch and pushed back the duvet, her fingers brushing the fresh grazes on her shins.

But it wasn't the beads of blood that made Granny Field suck in her breath, it was the sight of her own red and gold tail, lying crumpled in the bed.

"I brought it with me," Finch said, trying to straighten it out a little. "You have to put it on. You have to come back with me to the cloud and talk to Maverick."

Granny Field didn't answer immediately. Then she said, "Come on. Let's clean you up."

Finch tried to protest. She wanted to get going immediately, but Granny, who seemed a lot more like herself than when Finch had left her, insisted on bathing her grazes and on giving her food. She said Finch could fill her in while they waited for the kettle to boil and

that a cup of tea would help them both get their heads straight.

"Why didn't you ever tell me who you really were?" Finch crammed chunks of Granny's homemade bread into her mouth. She was ravenous after so much exercise and so many hours with nothing to eat but Maverick's skymallows.

"I wanted to tell. But I couldn't. I'd made a promise, you see." Granny Field set the tea tray down on the kitchen table next to the tail and Grandpa Field's walking stick. "I'd promised your grandpa." She rested her hand on the stick. "I'd promised Glen."

"But why?"

Granny stood the cups in their saucers. "I tried to tell him once, where I'd really come from that day when he found me in the field. I didn't remember myself at first. It must have been the shock of the fall but it all came back to me gradually."

"That's what Tomas said happened!" Finch said.

"Clever boy," Granny nodded. "Glen wouldn't have it though. Couldn't, or wouldn't, take it in. He said if I tried to tell anyone else they'd say I was deluded. Mad. He adored me, you see. And he was scared I'd be taken

164

away from him. It upset him dreadfully. So I promised never to talk about it again. I put it out of my mind. I loved my new life here so much I even almost stopped believing in the old one myself." She looked into Finch's eyes. "Until you came along, that is. As soon as you were born and I saw the soft pink in your hair, I knew. I meant to tell you one day. I know you've been confused sometimes about who you are, and I wanted to explain it to you so much. I was waiting for the right time, but I see now I left it too late. I've been a fool."

"But you couldn't have known something like this would happen."

"No. I couldn't." Granny Field shivered a little. "Poor Mav, though. I knew I must have hurt him. I knew he must have been wounded, but I always hoped he'd get over it, find someone new. It must have been awful, living with this boiling up inside him for all these years."

"It's still no excuse for what he's doing," Finch said. "He's so jealous of humans, he wants to damage us all. We've got to stop him, Granny. Tomas is trapped up there. We've got to rescue him and we've got to get the dreams back. Yours and everyone else's!"

She glanced towards the window. The sky was

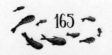

already changing from black to sombre grey. Dawn was on its way. She pushed back her chair.

"We have to go!" she said. "I've already stayed too long!" She didn't know what Maverick might do when he discovered her gone. She was worried he might take the dreams and Tomas far away, somewhere she could never find them. She snatched up the tail from the table. "Here, Granny. Put this on and let's go! When Maverick sees you in this, he'll remember who he is and stop. Maybe he'll find the good in himself all over again."

Granny Field looked at her, a bemused expression on her face.

"It's a bit torn, I know," Finch said, holding out the tail, "I must have caught it on the window latch, but we can tack it together. Where's your sewing basket? I'll fetch it. I'll thread the needle for you." The sight of the daylight seeping in at the windows made her heart beat faster again. She was suddenly more afraid than ever for Tomas and the dreams.

"Please," she said when Granny Field still didn't move. "We haven't much time!"

"Finch, love," Granny Field said gently. "I'm sorry

but there's no 'we' about it. I can never take this tail back. And I can't possibly come with you."

"But you have to. You have to make Maverick see he's wrong. Please. Only you can do that."

"You don't understand, love. My flying days are over. Long over."

"No!" Finch waved the tail at her. "We can fix it onto you somehow! We can!"

Granny Field shook her head. "I'm afraid not. I shed my tail when I came to earth." She fingered the soft feathery quills. "This is still pretty, but it's just a keepsake now. It's quite useless I'm afraid."

Finch felt tears smart in her eyes. The tail had been kept so well it seemed perfect, as if it really could be used to fly again. But it was stupid of her to believe it. She should have known. Maverick had rescued the tail but it was a souvenir and that was all. She let the tail fall.

"I'm earth-bound now," Granny Field went on. "A landlegger through and through." Then she raised Finch's chin in her fingers. "But you're not. You've no tail, but you can fly. You're the only person in the world who can."

Finch felt like burying her face in Granny's chest.

She had imagined Granny Field flying by her side, taking charge of the situation. But that wasn't going to happen. She couldn't bear to fly up to the cloud all by herself. How would she ever summon the energy? She didn't even feel like someone who could fly any more.

She swallowed as a terrible thought came to her.

"What if I can't do it again? What if Maverick sent his monster down while I was sleeping in your room? I fell asleep, Granny! He might have taken my flying dream away!"

"I don't think so," Granny Field said gently. "I would have seen it and there wasn't time. And even if it did come and take your dream, what difference can it make now? You know who you are Finch Field. You're part sky spirit and you can fly. You've proved it. Dream or no dream, that's the reality. You can fly any time you choose to. Nothing can take that away from you now."

Granny's eyes glittered and Finch saw what a strong person she was. She was so sure of herself, she was already recovering from the loss of her own dream. Maybe Finch could be like that too.

"Can I at least give Maverick a message from you," she said. "That might help."

168

"Ask him to remember who he is," Granny Field answered, taking Finch's hand and lacing her own rough fingers through it. "Sky spirits are givers and guardians of dreams. They don't take them away. Tell him he has to stop." She thought for a moment. "And tell him . . . tell him 'Seren says she's sorry.'"

"What if it doesn't do the trick?" Finch tried not to let her nerves get the better of her as Granny Field led her towards the front door.

"Then you'll find a different way. I've faith in you, Finch. You're the one link between two worlds. Now you go on. You'll be back soon with that boy, I know it. You'll come home, bringing all our dreams with you, and the sun too."

With that she kissed Finch on the forehead and pushed her gently outside.

Twenty-Two

In the garden Finch looked up. Daylight was coming and the cloud was clear to see. It was higher in the sky now and seemed so far away. Flying down had been one thing but how could she ever fly all the way up there?

She glanced round to see Granny Field still at the door, Philip in her arms. "Go!" she mouthed.

Finch knew she had no choice. Besides, she had promised Tomas. She started to run, skirting The Empress, her fingers brushing its papery bark as she passed. She wouldn't have the tree's help this time. She ran on down the path until she was going as fast as she could, leaped up over the gate and dived into the

dreary grey cloth of the waiting sky. She wondered for a moment if she would fall straight back down to earth. What if the flying gift was only a once-in-a-lifetime thing? What if now that she had touched the earth again she was no longer a bird girl, but had become a landlegger through and through, just like Granny?

She needn't have worried. The sky welcomed her in, just as deep water welcomes a strong swimmer. Finch forged her way upwards through soft air. She rose over the gloomy town, pulling back her arms strongly, pushing away all the old doubts, hurrying on.

Further down the coast, glimmers of orange and pale pink lit the dawn sky. She could see the hot air balloons being inflated ready for their morning flights. They wouldn't be flying over Sunview though. And they wouldn't again, not unless she could convince Maverick to take his awful cloud far, far away.

Climbing higher, Finch noticed that the cloud wasn't as still as usual. It seemed to be shaking. Something was going on in there, something bad! It had been so lovely being back in Granny Field's familiar kitchen but she had lingered too long. She kicked her legs hard, determined to reach the cloud. She didn't want Tomas

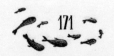

and the dreams thinking she had abandoned them.

As she flew closer, the air around her grew thinner and it was harder to breathe. The cloud looked increasingly unsteady. By the time she reached it, it was rocking, tilting sharply from side to side, looking set to turn right over like a capsizing ship. Pedalling air with her feet, Finch used her hands to feel her way along the bottom of the swaying cloud, until she found the remains of the hole she had used to leave it by. Quickly she swam up into it.

She couldn't work out what was going on at first. The dreams had all come loose and were rolling around, scuffing up the misty floor so that it billowed about like storm-churned sand. Finch couldn't see Maverick anywhere. But she could hear him roaring.

"Try to trick me, would you?" he shouted.

Tomas came staggering through the mist, dodging as he ran. Maverick swooped after him. He had a rope, coiled like a lasso above his head and he was swinging it, preparing to fling it over Tomas.

"You helped her escape, didn't you? My prize! My perfect revenge!" His feathers crackled with anger. "You'll pay for this, landlegger!"

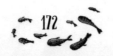

Tomas was so scrawny, he wasn't a very fast runner. Maverick should have caught him easily but the dreams kept getting in his way. The kookaburra flew, pecking at his eyes; the wellington boots kicked at his shins; Dave's wave and the bowling balls rolled in front of him, trying to trip him up or knock him down.

"Out of my way!" Maverick screamed at the big friendly face of Prince Fred, which, still smiling, loomed in front of him, blocking his view of Tomas. Finch wondered how long this had been going on for. Poor Tomas was slowing down, wheezing. He looked totally drained. She should have come back sooner!

She bowed her head, scrunched up her fists and tried to think. She was going to talk to Maverick, but if she couldn't persuade him with words alone, she was going to need a back-up plan.

She noticed she was standing on the fishing net that had held the dreams. It lay spread out on the cloud floor. Seeing it like that, all slack and empty, gave her the seed of an idea.

"Stop!" she shouted at Maverick. "Leave him alone. It's not his fault. Stop, everyone. Please stop. I'm back. I'm here!"

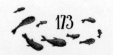

Everything ground to a halt. The murk cleared and Finch found herself face to face with Maverick once again.

"Well, well, well," he said, letting his lasso drop. "You've come back."

"Yes, I have," Finch said. "But not to stay. I came back to . . . to give you a chance."

Maverick folded his arms, a smirk playing on his lips. "Oh I see. It's like that, is it? What do you mean, 'a chance'?"

"A chance to redeem yourself. A chance to put things right. Granny Field – Serendipity – asks you to remember who you really are. To remember the good in yourself."

Maverick froze at the mention of Granny Field.

"And what exactly does Serendipity know about who I am," he said in a voice as brittle as icicles. "She, who hasn't thought of me for decades!"

"She's sorry about that," Finch said. "She really is. But don't you see? You can still undo the damage you've done." Aware that Tomas was slumped on the pillows, looking ready to faint, she spoke quickly. "Please. It's not too late. Lower the cloud over The

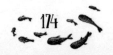
174

Empress again now. Tomas and I will climb down. We'll take the dreams with us and return them to their owners. They're no use to you, you've proved that already. All you're doing is hurting people. And I don't think you really want to do that. I don't think you are truly evil. You made a monster but that doesn't mean you are one. Granny Field told me how kind and gentle you used to be."

Maverick brushed an arm across his head. He was trying to hide it, but she could tell her words had shaken him.

"Serendipity said that about me?" he murmured.

"Yes," Finch went on. "She said you were her childhood love, and that nothing that's happened, nothing either of you have done can take that away. She asks you to break up this cloud and let Sunview be the place it was before. She asks you to let Tomas, and me, her grandchild, go."

Maverick's face suddenly hardened to stone. "And if I do that, if I let you go, what do you think will happen to me then? What the devil should I do with myself?"

Finch hadn't thought about that. She shrugged. "Can't you go back to doing whatever you used to do?

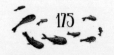

Scattering dream dust, giving people new dreams?"

Maverick flapped his coat-tails at her. "Impossible!" he snorted. "The Cloud Council would never allow it. They expelled me from the workforce years ago. Banished me from their sight. I have no one to be with now, and no home to go to. I only have my project, my grand scheme. I have my monster," he opened his arms wide, "and I have this cloud. If I give it up I will have nothing. Nothing and nowhere!"

"You could come with us." Tomas propped himself up on the pillows. He was still trying to catch his rasping breath. His skin was waxy and his eyes looked worryingly large and dark.

"That's a brilliant idea, Tomas." Finch turned to Maverick. "Why not? You could come to earth and see Serendipity again. She can't fly up here without her tail, but you could fly down to her. Why not come to earth with us?"

For a moment she thought Maverick was actually giving it some serious thought but then he turned on her, sneering, "And be consigned to live down there? In the mud? As a useless landlegger?" He spat into the air and shrieked, "I'd rather die!"

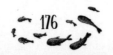

He flew to the pillows, pushed Tomas off them, and began tearing at them with his claw-like hands. He ripped their covers apart and pulled out handfuls of yellow powder, showering it over his shoulders, again and again, until the pillows were empty and the cloud awash with shining dust.

Seeing Maverick destroying the pillows, Finch realised it was useless trying to persuade him to see sense. He was too far gone for that. Meanwhile, the seed of a plan that had sown itself in her head was growing. It wasn't a perfect plan, but it was the only one she had. It would have to do. Quickly she knelt down and raised the fishing net above her head.

"Very well," she said, sounding as meek as possible. "Perhaps you're right. You were treated badly and someone has to pay. Tomas and I are the sacrifice. It's like you told us before, we'll just have to accept it. Come on everyone," she said to the dreams. "Get back in your net." She held the net up, gesturing for the dreams to go back inside it.

"Finch?" Tomas looked at her questioningly.

"Stay where you are, Tomas," she said, avoiding his eye. "This is what Maverick our sky spirit master wants.

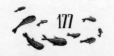

I, Finch Field, am part sky spirit too, and . . . and I command you to do as he says."

Slowly, hesitantly, the dreams began to obey her. They floated one at a time into the net, letting her wrap it around them. As the net filled, it began to swell, until it was shaped like an enormous flower bulb.

Out of the corner of her eye, she could see Tomas looking puzzled, but she couldn't help that now.

"So. Seeing it my way at last, are we?" Maverick flitted from side to side. She knew he was suspicious but he also seemed pleased.

"Yes," Finch answered quietly. "Actions have consequences. I see that now." As she spoke, she kept on finding spaces for the dreams filling the net. They were almost all inside. Only Delia's boots hung back reluctantly and had to be encouraged by the kookaburra, which nudged them in with its beak. Once they were all in, Finch quickly gathered up the ends and twisted them into a knot. "Tomas," she said, keeping her tone brisk and sharp, although inside she was trembling with fear. "Come and hold onto the dreams so they can't escape again and be a nuisance to our new master." She stared at him hard, willing him not to argue.

Tomas got to his feet, and met her gaze. She needn't have worried. As their eyes locked it was as if a bolt of electrical energy passed between them, and she knew he understood. Without a word he stepped over to her and she passed him the knot.

"Be sure to hold them good and tight!" she ordered. "Don't let go for a second!" Then she took hold of the slack end of the net.

Maverick was delighted. He laughed and clapped his hands, convinced he had won.

"That's more like it," he cried, suddenly speeding away to his private chamber. "That's the attitude!"

Quickly, Finch slipped off her cardigan and wrapped the end of the net that held the dreams around her middle.

She was still tying her cardigan sleeves around her waist when Maverick came swooping back, carrying a huge cloth map which he unfolded, flapping it open in the air. "This is more like it," he said. "I knew you'd come round to my way of thinking, child. You shall be my companions now, my own little helpers. Now we're ready. We'll leave this place. We'll go and take over a whole new town, drain out more dreams!" He bent over

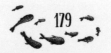

the map. "Where shall we travel to first?"

Finch was standing so close to Tomas she could feel his breath on the back of her head. "Jump!" she breathed.

Finch started jumping up and down. Tomas did too. Maverick didn't notice at first.

"What's that?" he asked, busy with the map. "Where, my little bird girl? Where did you say you would you like to go first?"

"Home!" Finch cried the instant he looked up. "I'm not your bird girl, and I want to go home! Now jump, Tomas! Jump! Jump for all you're worth!"

Twenty-Three

The two of them jumped up and down madly, the net clenched tightly in their hands. Finch was sure she could feel the floor weaken under her stamping but it wasn't happening nearly quickly enough.

"Harder!" she shouted. "Jump harder!"

Maverick's face fell. "What trickery is this?" He dropped the map and surged towards them, bellowing. "What do the pair of you think—"

Finch didn't catch the rest, because at that moment the floor fell away. All she did hear was Tomas crying out in alarm as they tumbled out of the cloud.

"Finch!" Terror shook his voice. She hadn't had time

to consider how he would feel out in the sky without even a safety harness.

"Hold on to the net!" she cried. "Just hold on! That's all you have to do, Tomas, I promise. I'll do the rest!" Praying he would be strong enough, she swam outwards into the air. It was hard work — like swimming against a strong current — but checking back, she saw that her plan was working. The dreams were floating up above her in their net, just like a hot air balloon, with Tomas clinging on below. She wished he could be in a basket like the ones beneath real hot air balloons, but this was the very best she could manage.

There was no sign of Maverick, but she felt sure he would chase them. She had to keep flying, even more strongly than before. She had to bring her precious cargo safely in to land. But despite the kookaburra flapping its wings as hard as it could inside the netting, Tomas and the dreams were heavy to tow and she couldn't make nearly such quick progress as when she was flying alone.

As they made their painfully slow descent, the dawn light widened. The roofs of Sunview were tinged with morning purple. The shadowy shapes of the town

buildings gradually came into focus. When the beach appeared beneath her, Finch was astonished to see it had letters on it. Huge red and gold letters spread right across the sand like flames.

FORGIVE

The message had been made out of tail feathers. Granny Field must have got to work with her dressmaking scissors as soon as Finch had left her. She had cut her tail into a thousand pieces and brought them to the beach to lay out on the sea-smoothed sand. It would never be a tail again.

Finch remembered Maverick ranting, "Take it back, take it back!" Had he secretly been hoping to see Granny in her old tail again? Even he would know that was impossible now.

"Look, Tomas!" Finch called. "Look at that!"

If Tomas answered her at all his words were drowned out by a long low moan. Was that Maverick she wondered, or just the wind getting up at last? And was that Granny Field herself she could see on the sand, next to what was left of her sky spirit tail, her arms

raised to the sky? It was! Could Maverick see her too?

She was still straining to see when Tomas cried out.

"Finch!" His voice travelled only faintly through the air, but she could tell he was distressed. "I can't . . . I can't feel my fingers."

"Just another minute," she called back. Why couldn't she fly faster? "I'll soon have you down on the beach. Keep holding on."

She gritted her teeth and was gathering herself to fly harder, when she heard a gentle, "Oh!"

She looked back just in time to see Tomas drop from the net. Her heart lunged.

He fell so simply, with his arms up above his head. He looked like a boy jumping on a trampoline, but he was never going to bounce up again. He was only going down, and there was no soft landing waiting for him. Just the deep cold grey sea.

Finch was stunned. Before she even had a chance to think what to do, there was a streak of silver and blue, and Maverick, appearing from nowhere, flew past her and straight into Tomas. She saw him seize Tomas's shoulders in fury, forcing him downward, even faster than before. Tomas clutched at him in panic and the

two of them went spinning and rolling through the sky, and disappeared.

"Tomas!" Finch screamed. "Tomas!" There was no answering call. She looked around wildly but there was no sign of Tomas, or Maverick either.

They must already be in the sea.

Her breath came sharply and felt jagged in her chest. She had heard no splash but she could imagine the speed at which the two of them must have hit the water. Even if either of them could swim, she knew they would never survive such a fall.

Finch hovered helplessly in the air. The rescue attempt was a disaster. She had let Tomas go. It was all her fault. She rolled herself into a ball. She couldn't go on. She couldn't!

"Tomas!" she cried. "Tomas! Where is he?" She uncurled again and screamed up at the dreams. "Where is he?"

The dreams looked bemused as if they'd like to answer her but didn't know what to say. Even the ever-smiling Prince Fred seemed dismayed. They looked almost guilty, as if it was their fault that Tomas had fallen.

But of course the dreams weren't to blame. They were innocent victims, just like Tomas.

Above them the dark cloud began to bend and break up. A breeze was starting to blow.

"I'm sorry," Finch said, her eyes smarting with tears. "I'm so sorry!" She hardly knew who she was apologising to – the dreams for shouting at them, or Tomas for letting him fall.

The chimneys of the fishermen's cottages and the white roof of the bowling pavilion were gleaming up at her. Sunlight washed over Sunview-on-Sea. It was starting to look brighter, like itself again, and Finch knew she had the power to help it recover even more.

She looked again at the dreams, shaking away her tears.

"Please," she said. "Let me take you home."

At least she could do that. She was the only person who could do it too. She was the only person in the world who could both walk and fly, the only girl in the world who was part human, part sky spirit. She knew that now, and knowing it made her feel very, very lonely.

Because she had lost Tomas. And that was the worst thing in the world.

Winding the dangling net around her shoulders, she sighed, heavily, shakily. The dreams needed her to do this. Tomas would have wanted her to do it too. Forcing herself to make one last effort, she swooped and dived for the beach.

Twenty-Four

F inch hardly noticed her feet touching down on the solid damp sand. She made her way up the beach, pulling the dream balloon along behind her. She scarcely felt the breeze lifting the red and gold feathers so that they flickered and danced at her ankles. She walked straight to where Granny Field was standing by the jetty.

Letting out a single sob, she allowed herself to be pulled into her granny's waiting arms.

"They're gone, Granny," Finch said.

"Yes, I know. I saw them falling." Granny Field held her still more tightly.

"Should we swim out to look? Find the spot? Should we call the coastguard? Do you think they could have . . . They might . . ." Her words trailed away as Granny shook her head.

"No one could come back from that, love," Her eyes were watery and her expression very grave. She swallowed and said, "I shall have to tell Irena."

"Yes." Finch felt sick. "But how? How will you explain it all, everything that's happened?"

Granny Field stroked Finch's hair. "I don't know, darling. I'll find a way."

They stood very still, staring out to sea. Nothing disturbed the surface of the water. Tomas and Maverick must have sunk down so deep. There was no trace of them, no chance of rescuing them. The sea had swallowed them and now it rolled on as always, as if they had never even existed. Finch clung to Granny Field. It was the most dreadful thing that had ever happened.

Even Philip knew better than to bark or romp about. As the three of them stood there a shaft of brilliant sunlight broke through the sky, lighting up a million golden particles of dust that hung sparkling in the air.

"Dream dust," Finch whispered as they watched it fall.

Then they pulled apart. They took the dream net between them and began walking up the jetty. Whatever their feelings, they still had an urgent job to do. People had been sleeping late in Sunview recently but they would all be waking up soon.

As soon as they left the beach the dreams became restive, jostling inside the net, jockeying for position. Finch realised they sensed they were close to home and were eager to be released.

"Off you go, then," she said, stopping to pull open a flap in the netting.

The big catch of sea fish was the first to leave. The fish swam out and whipped away, over the harbour wall towards the fishermen's cottages, squeezing themselves in through gaps in the bedroom windows.

Then, as if it was in an enormous hurry, Granny Field's garden dream pressed its way right down through the net and shot out and upwards. It flowed all around Granny Field and melted back into her, absorbed right through her skin. Granny Field nodded slowly. A moment before she had seemed blurry to

Finch, like an out of focus photograph, but now she was completely herself again, sharp-edged, clear, and very sad.

"Work to be done," she said briskly, taking Finch's hand.

They trudged through the town, watching the dreams fly out one at a time, making their way safely back to their sleeping owners. When they passed Dave's flat, Finch stopped to watch the koala and the kookaburra ride the great wave out of the net and into Dave's letterbox. At least Dave would have his dream back. It was good to know he could start saving for the Down Under fund again.

"Better keep going," Granny Field said. The sun was getting stronger and warmer by the second. They quickened their pace.

As they walked up Middle Street, the bowling balls and the trophy danced up over Fred's Fish shop and down through his chimney. Delia's red and yellow boots jumped out with them and skipped away up the hill. Then the big friendly face Finch had named Prince Fred slipped out of the net.

"Who do you belong to, then?" she asked. The Fred

face only winked its farewell, and floated on its back, up and between the curtains of Souvenir Sue's bedroom window. Its crown was the last part of it to disappear.

"Sue's prince," Finch whispered. "Of course."

The curtains waved and fluttered back at her. Fresh new air wafted through the town. It would have made Finch feel so good if only her heart wasn't so heavy.

The last dream to go was Irena's. The still-splendid sponge cakes and glossy buns bounced and rolled their way through the air vent at the Conch Café. Finch bent and touched the vent. It still smelled of cigarette smoke. Irena would have her dream back now, but what use would that be without Tomas, her real live nephew?

"She won't be worried yet," Finch turned to Granny Field. "He told her he was coming to Hilltop House."

Granny Field nodded sadly. "I'll talk to her now," she said. "I'll tell her the whole story. She has a right to know."

"I can't stay." Finch felt herself choke with tears. She couldn't bear it. "I can't stay and hear that. I'm sorry, Granny!"

The tears she'd held back suddenly flew out of her eyes. They kept on coming too. She couldn't remember

crying like this ever before. She'd never felt such strong emotion in all her life. It bowled her over, as overwhelming as an ocean breaker on a windy day.

"I'm so sorry!"

"You've nothing to be sorry for, Finch." Granny Field took her hands. "And it's not your fault," she said. "You must remember that. Whatever's happened, it's not your responsibility. It's Maverick's. And mine. I'll deal with whatever happens now. You don't have to."

Granny Field gently turned her so that she was looking down over the town again. The sky was blue now. The sun was up properly and Maverick's cloud had completely evaporated. Sunview-on-Sea was sparkling like the sea itself and Finch could hear jolly and excited voices calling good mornings to one another.

"That's the sound of happiness and hope down there," Granny Field said. "The people of Sunview can dream again. They'll never know it, but that's your doing, Finch Field. That's something to be very proud of."

"Not just my doing," Finch said quickly. "Tomas's too. If he hadn't suggested it, I never would have tried to fly. I never would have known." She bit her lip,

thinking how she hadn't even had a chance to thank him for that.

"You need some rest." Granny touched her face lightly with her fingers. "You're shattered. Why don't you go on home? Take Philip with you and go to bed for a while."

"I can't." How could she lie down and sleep as if none of this had ever happened? It would be impossible. But she couldn't stay to hear Granny Field break the news to Irena either. She had to keep moving. "I'll go for a walk," she said. "I'll see you later on."

"Stay here, Philip!" she ordered. The dog had been sitting next to Granny Field but now was skipping round her legs, eager to comfort her, to go with her. She didn't feel like taking him though. This wasn't just an ordinary day for an ordinary dog walk. She couldn't just do normal things, not now.

She headed off alone, back down the hill. She was dimly aware of a bustle going on around her as shutters rattled up, shop doorbells rang, people whistled snatches of tunes, yawning loudly and stretching sleep away, joking and laughing.

"Someone's up with the lark!"

194

Souvenir Sue and Fred from the fish shop were blocking her path. They were holding hands across the narrow stream that separated their two shops.

"Oh, Finch!" Sue said. "You'll never guess. Fred's just asked me to marry him, and I've said yes! I always knew my prince would come one day but whoever would have guessed he'd be coming from so close by?" She laughed as Fred doffed his straw hat, took the plastic daffodil from its brim and handed it to her.

"I've held a torch for you, Susan, for a very long time," he said. "And today, don't ask me why, I suddenly found it in me to pluck up the courage and tell you." He winked. "Must be something in the air, eh, young Finch?"

Finch managed a half smile. "I suppose so."

"Hey, it's nothing to cry about," Sue exclaimed, pulling her hanky out from her cardigan sleeve. She dabbed Finch's eyes and then her own. "Here, you've set me off now, too."

"Sorry," Finch said. "And congratulations! Excuse me though."

She ducked under Sue and Freds' arms and ran on. She didn't stop for anyone else, not even Dave, who

came out of his flat and said "G'day, Finch," in his best and cheeriest Australian accent. She gave him a wave; she was glad he was back to normal, but she couldn't have a conversation with him now. She carried on running all the way to the beach.

People were already laying out towels and setting up stripy windbreaks on the sand. She should have been pleased as she picked her way between them. This was what she had wanted. Although there were all these people around her she had never felt so alone in her life. She had found out who and what she was at last, but she realised there was only one person she wanted to talk to about it. The one person apart from Granny Field who would have understood everything.

But Tomas was gone.

She hurried on, heading up onto the coast path. She kept walking until she was on the Camels. Finally, she sat down at the cliff edge and stared out over the sparkling ocean.

All she could think about was Tomas, and her last sight of him: twined together with Maverick in the sky, in that terrible embrace.

Twenty-Five

Finch stayed near the cliff edge for a long while. She didn't know how long because she had lost all track of time. It hardly seemed important.

It was a relief to be away from the beach. Below her, more and more people were arriving on the golden sand. She could hear the thrilled squeals of children, already playing in the water. Bright sunlight bounced off all the differently coloured cars streaming back into the harbour car park. Further off she could see Sue and Fred, squeezed together on the seat of Fred's ride-on mower as they cut the grass of the bowling green. Fred's high standards had returned along with his dreams.

Sunview-on-Sea was back to normal. Everyone in it was happy again. Almost everyone. Finch was glad for them but she couldn't be happy too. She wished she could be a proper part of things, and feel what everyone else was feeling, but she knew she couldn't. Not without Tomas.

Shielding her eyes to see the fishing boats motoring out over the gently undulating sea, it dawned on her that Philip was barking. She had been dimly aware that he hadn't stayed with Granny Field as she had told him to, but had trotted after her, keeping a little distance between them all the way through the town. He must have followed her all the way up here, too.

"Quiet boy," she said, her eyes still fixed on the sea. "Quiet down!"

But Philip didn't quieten. He barked louder and more insistently until he was impossible to ignore. Finch sighed. "What are you doing, Philip?" He had jumped up on the old pill box, yapping, whining, and yapping again. "It's just some rabbit," she said. "Let it go." The terrified creature must be hiding in the mound of moss and heather that covered the pill box.

"Leave it!" she shouted at Philip who was still

barking. Frustrated with him, and with herself for shouting at him, Finch was about to turn away again when something white caught her eye.

Her heart jolted.

An arm.

A thin white arm, reaching out of the bracken. Its hand lay open, palm upwards, the fingers spread lifelessly. She recognised the pale fingernails at once; they were bitten right down to the quick.

"Tomas," she whispered, and felt her forehead go clammy and cold. "Tomas. Oh, Tomas!" He hadn't fallen into the sea after all, but onto the clifftop. She didn't know which was worse.

Philip whimpered and licked the fingers. Then he howled.

Finch sank to her knees and buried her face in her hands. She felt like howling too. Poor Tomas! Poor Irena! The worst really had happened. And it was all her fault. She should have found a different way out of the cloud, a safer one. Granny Field said she wasn't responsible, but she was.

"It's all my fault!" she sobbed. "All my fault!"

"What is all your fault?"

Finch whirled round, wondering who had spoken so close to her ear. Someone must have crept up on her.

But there was no one on the cliff path. The voice was coming from the pill box itself.

"What did you do wrong?"

She knew that voice. It was hoarse and soft both at once.

Hardly daring to believe what her ears were telling her, Finch turned to see Tomas, sitting up in the bracken and smiling his crooked smile.

"What did you do wrong exactly? Why is your dog wailing? And why are you opening and closing your mouth like a fish who is stranded out of the water?"

"You're . . . alive!" Finch managed to stammer. "Are you . . . all right?"

"I believe I am," Tomas said, sitting up and examining his arms and flexing his legs. "Everything seems to be in order, more or less. No bone is broken."

"But, how? It's impossible . . ." She stopped. Relief flooded through her and she didn't know whether to laugh or cry. But she couldn't see how Tomas could possibly have survived such a long fall. The green

growth on top of the pill box was deep, but not deep enough to break a fall from the sky.

"It's not often I see you short of words, Finch Field," Tomas said. "But if you're wondering about the reason I am all present and correct, perhaps it has to do with this." He reached behind him and pulled out something shiny, silvery and blue.

Finch recognised it at once. She took one end from Tomas and they held it between them. It flapped in the breeze, like washing on a line, gleaming and glittering in the sunshine. "Maverick's tail!"

Tomas said, "I think your sky spirit has saved my life."

"Not *my* sky spirit," Finch said quickly. "But I don't get it. He was trying to kill you. I saw him dive at you. He sent you spinning to the ground. He wanted to smash you to smithereens."

"No." Tomas stroked the tail thoughtfully. "I think he did want to do that at first. His face was full of anger when he grabbed me. His fists too. And yes, we did go spinning. But then he saw the message in the sand."

"Granny Field's message?"

"Yes. He saw that tail, all split in pieces, and he cried

out as if he was in great pain. Then something changed. We came out of the spin. Maverick lay on his back in the sky and he held me, like this," Tomas cupped his hand round his chin, "like a lifeguard at the swimming pool. He must have brought me down to earth like that."

"And he hit the ground before you. Maverick broke your fall with his own body!" He really did have a heart, like Granny Field had said. "He remembered the good in himself after all."

"Maybe." Now it was Tomas's turn to be bewildered. "I don't remember anything else." He ran a hand through his spiky hair. "But I will tell you this, I've just had the best sleep I've ever had. As sound as a log!"

He grinned suddenly and Finch found herself grinning back. She was so happy to see him smiling and well, she almost felt like launching herself at him and hugging him.

"What?" she said instead. "What are you grinning about?"

Tomas shook his head, as if he'd decided against telling her. "Being unconscious is not all bad, I think. It gave me a good rest anyway. I feel one thousand times better than I did before."

He did look better. His face was less drawn, and the hollows under his eyes weren't quite so deep. Thanks to the sun, he was even getting a few freckles on his nose.

A gust of wind rippled Maverick's blue tail and it whirred as if there was still life in it.

"Where is he now?" Finch said. "Did he die in the fall? Is that why his tail is here and he isn't? Is Maverick dead?"

"Actually, I don't think so," Tomas said slowly. He picked something out of his lap. A paper bag, empty now of skymallows. Finch recognised the spidery handwriting on it. "'*I may forgive,*'" she read aloud, "'*but I will never forget.*' It's a message for Granny Field!" She took the bag from Tomas and read on. "'*And if I should dream a dream in this dreadful domain of landleggers, you may be sure it will be only of you*'."

"Huh! Is that his way of saying sorry? The best he could do?"

"Perhaps for now." Tomas said. "In any case you should probably give the note to your grandmother." Then he pointed. "Finch! Look over there!"

Finch turned to follow the line of his finger. The green humps of The Three Camels stretched away

203

from them. On the farthest hump was a figure. A small bandy-legged man scurried along with his back to them. He was tottering awkwardly, as if he didn't trust his new legs to carry him; his beard flew out behind him and the tails of his long coat flapped against his knees.

"He's a proper landlegger now, I think." Tomas began hauling himself down from the pill box, while Philip snuffled happily at his socks.

"He won't like that. He hates landleggers." Finch offered him her hand.

Tomas took it and held onto it. "Maybe he'll see the good in them eventually. Most people aren't so bad. Are they, Finch Field? Not if you give them a chance? If you don't jump to conclusions."

Finch felt herself blushing hotly. She knew Tomas was referring to the way she had jumped to a conclusion about him when they had first met. "No," she agreed. "Lots of landleggers are really . . . quite nice. And they make very good friends."

"I see."

"Especially when they stop throwing stones!" she added, wriggling her hand out of his and turning away

because she could suddenly feel herself starting to blush again.

"Do you know what?" Tomas said, not appearing to notice and brushing fern leaves from his shorts.

"What?" said Finch, as they began to walk down the cliff path.

"I had a dream myself while I was sleeping back there. A proper long one."

"Did you?"

"Yes. And it was a truly excellent dream. With all sorts of detail." Tomas paused. "Don't you want to know what it was about?"

"All right."

"It was a dream about you."

Secretly pleased, Finch bit her lip. "Really?"

"Yes. Really. I was in it too, of course. I was a bit taller than I am now. A bit plumper too. So were you as a matter of fact." Finch gave him a shove. "And we were both here in Sunview-on-Sea for the long summer holiday. We looked pretty good actually."

"What were we doing?" Finch kept her eyes on the path, trying not to sound too interested.

"Oh, all sorts of things. Swimming in the sea, playing

205

on the beach, walking on these Camels. When we weren't doing all that we were helping Aunt Irena with her fancy new bakery. And then we were camping in a tent in the most beautiful garden I have ever seen. A garden with an enormous tree, a pond like a lake, and a view over town all the way to the sea."

"That's Hilltop House!" Finch said. Tomas was describing Granny Field's garden. The garden of her dreams. She would be able to make it now, too. And now Finch had found Tomas, everyone, even Irena, was going to be all right.

"It really was a good dream," Tomas said. "The first one I can remember having in years too. Do you think it might come true?"

Finch smiled and impulsively linked an arm through his. "Yes," she said. "I actually think it might."

A hot air balloon, the one patterned like a rainbow, sailed over their heads.

"The balloons are back!" Finch cried and they paused to wave at the excited passengers who were calling out to them.

"Tomas?" Finch said, giving him a sideways look when the balloon had gone by. "Do you think I'm strange?"

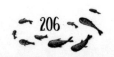

"What?"

"Do you think I'm strange? A weirdo, I mean. That's what they call me at school. Do you think I have feathers for brains, too?"

"Hmm. You? Weird?" He studied her as if he was considering the matter seriously. After a time he shook his head. "No," he said. "You seem quite ordinary to me. Quite normal. In fact," he added with a grin, "you're so normal I'd say you're practically dull!"

"Cheek!" Finch cried, although really she was delighted with his answer. She felt a sudden urge to run as fast as she could. She yanked Tomas's arm and pulled him along with her. The two of them charged as quickly as they dared down the steep path, with Philip dashing between their legs and yapping, wild with joy.

Finch didn't know, as she ran, if she would ever dream of flying again or if she would ever really fly again. And at this moment she didn't care. Because running down the hill with Tomas, laughing and shrieking, on their way to the place and the people she loved, was so good. It made her so happy.

It felt exactly like flying anyway.